Distant Voices

Distant Voices

MAEVE FRIEL

POOLBEG

Published in 1994 by
Poolbeg,
A division of Poolbeg Enterprises Ltd,
Knocksedan House,
123 Baldoyle Industrial Estate,
Dublin 13, Ireland

© Maeve Friel 1994

The moral right of the author has been asserted.

The Publishers gratefully acknowledge the assistance of
The Northern Ireland Arts Council.

A catalogue record for this book is available from the British Library.

ISBN 1 85371 410 0

Cover illustration by Alex Callaway
Cover design by Poolbeg Group Services Ltd
Set by Poolbeg Group Services Ltd in Garamond 10.5/13.5
Printed by The Guernsey Press Company Ltd,
Vale, Guernsey, Channel Islands.

To Joe Kennedy & Clare Nicell

A Note on the Author

Maeve Friel was born in Derry and educated in Dublin. *Distant Voices* is her third book for children. Other books include *Charlie's Story*, and *The Deerstone* which was short-listed for the ICBT/Bisto Book of the Year Award. Ms Friel is currently working on both an adult and a children's novel.

Praise for *Charlie's Story*

"Disturbing and compelling."
Madeleine Keane, *Sunday Independent*

" . . . an impressively courageous novel which confronts many important themes without ever resorting to the obvious, the mundane or the predictable."
Children's Books Ireland

Chapter 1

A fleet of the foreigners came into Lough Foyle . . .
Cennrig was quickly abandoned by them, except for a
few who remained behind in it through sloth . . .
Fergal, son of Domnall, King of the North, was in
hostilities with them, and killed the crew of one of their
ships and took its booty.

The Annals of Ulster, 920 AD

Only you will know where to find me.

Ellie opened her eyes. A tall boy-man was standing at
her bedroom window, his slim face and golden hair
caught in a pool of ghostly green moonlight.

My name is Harald Olafsson, he said, turning to face
her with his startling blue eyes. *You must give me leave
to speak to you. You have no need to fear me.*

Ellie raised her head from her pillow and rubbed her
eyes. Was someone there or was she still dreaming? The
boy looked at her, his expression so sad and wretched
that she felt she must reach out and comfort him, but
the figure floated out into the starry night without
another word.

Night-time had always been vividly alive for Ellie –
her dreams came thick and fast as soon as she hit the

1

pillow and continued through the night until the first proop-proop of the alarm clock woke her. Some nights the familiar faces of her family and friends were crowded out by less well-known ones, people on the margins of her life like shop assistants, dimly remembered faces from her childhood, even, sometimes, the casualties of the random bombings and murders that fleeted across the television screen nightly – she imagined her brain frantically sifting through her life each night, recording everything, filing it all away for posterity.

Recently though, something strange and puzzling was happening – her dreams were so different they felt alien, out of character. It was almost as if they didn't belong to her. This voice, this Harald, was haunting her dreams, speaking to her in his strange accent, drawing her into another life, forcing her to listen . . . She began to feel as if he had burrowed beneath her skin and was using her sleep to spin dreams thronged with strange men from long ago, their distant voices straining to be heard.

Each night now, for over a week, she had been dreaming of a ship, following its journey across the ocean. It came, she knew, from a wild and barren place, sailing swiftly across the sea where whales loomed and large seabirds circled and screamed above the sails. Harald stood next to the captain at the rudder. He was tall and broad-shouldered but his long slim face was still clean-shaven, with just a sprinkling of fine hairs on his upper lip. He had blond hair, so pale it was almost white, which he wore held back at the nape of his neck in a long ponytail. On the seventh night, he smiled and stretched out an arm to take her hand, but she shrank away from his touch and opened her eyes. The figure stood by the window, beckoning to her, as real and life-like as the figure in her dream, but as she raised her head from the pillow, he floated out into the night.

Ellie fell back into a fitful sleep, drifting in and out of dreams. Several times the scene shifted to a wide sandy beach, a place she half recognised but could not name. It was pitch-black to begin with but as her eyes became used to the darkness, she made out a crowd of people moving across the sand dunes. There was a high wind howling, stirring up the sea into white horses, making her shiver even in sleep. The tide was coming in fast, throwing itself against the cliff in thunderous bursts of spray.

Ellie was floating, looking down on the strand as if she were drifting above it in a hot-air balloon, conscious that at any moment she might come crashing down to earth. Suddenly great tongues of orange fire lit up the whole beach and the sand dunes behind. A vast bonfire had been set ablaze on the shore. In the flames Ellie could make out the dark shape of a ship around which the strange figures danced and ran, many of them wailing and crying out in a language she could not understand. A number of men approached the ship, carrying wooden shields which they beat with long sticks to drown the wailing of the dancing women. Others began to move forward, each bearing a burning piece of wood which they threw on the pyre. The wind grew stronger and more terrifying, fanning the fire on the ship so that the blazing timbers creaked and groaned. Deep in sleep, Ellie's hand brushed her cheek to wipe away the splinters of sooty wood which the wind carried across the beach. The air was thick with the smell of burning resin and the salt of the sea.

She struggled to wake, and lay tossing and turning in her bed, listening to the wind howling outside and rattling the window panes. She heard the Guildhall clock strike five o'clock, then the quarter hour and the half hour. Some time later she must have drifted back to sleep only to take up the dream where it had ended.

The burning ship had turned to ash. She began to walk towards it, feeling underfoot the spiky blades of marram grass pricking her bare feet. As she drew closer, the heat coming off the charred timbers burned her cheeks and scorched the back of her throat so that she stopped and raised a hand to shield her face. She was astonished to find her cheeks wet with tears.

You're not dreaming any more, whispered the voice of Harald. *Come and find me*, he said. *Only you will know where to look.*

Once more Ellie forced herself to waken up: she *would* not listen any longer to the voice. At first she lay buried beneath the duvet, too scared to look into the room for fear of what she might see – but the voice would not go away. It called her name, repeating it again and again in a soothing hypnotic tone until finally she could ignore it no longer. She slipped out of bed and moved, trance-like, to the window.

Not a being stirred in the city. She looked down on the river, full and grey in the early morning light. It was moving swiftly, engorged by the recent heavy rains so that it almost lapped the lower deck of the bridge, and swelling in a wide s-shaped curve as it passed out of the city towards the lough beyond. As she watched, her blood froze.

A spectral fleet of six sailing ships was advancing up

the river. Each bore one huge square sail behind which the wind screamed. They glided over the surface of the water like a group of monstrous invincible swans but as they came closer, Ellie could see that the long necks of their prows ended not in the graceful head of a bird, but in the snarling, bare-toothed sneer of dogs and dragons.

Am I still dreaming, she thought. Is this a dream within a dream? She shut her eyes tightly and wished herself back into consciousness. No, she was not dreaming any more. Gingerly she drew the side of her hand across the cold wet condensation on the windowpane and peered through the smear. The ships were still there and coming closer. She blinked again to make the image fade and rubbed her eyes. The city on the other side of the river seemed to shimmer in the light and fade away. The quays, the bridge, the cathedral spires disappeared. Now the soft rounded hills behind grew darker and more wooded. The familiar landscape that Ellie had grown up with, the contours and shadows of the city she had looked across at every day since she had been old enough to be aware of the world outside her window, seemed to shrink. Finally all that was left was a cluster of low buildings perched on one hill with the river circling around them. The modern city had vanished, leaving nothing but the island in the middle of the river.

I am dreaming, thought Ellie, even though I think I am not. She turned back: her room was exactly as she expected – the duvet lying at the base of the bed where she had flung it, the walls lined with the faces of musicians and actors, the green hands of the alarm clock showing ten to six. She put her face close up against the window and stared out into the darkness.

Down on the river below the ships sailed relentlessly towards the city on its tiny island.

As Ellie looked on transfixed, two cormorants, flying in low over the water, landed on a rock mid-stream and stretched their stiff black wings, spreading them out to dry, like two witches of the sea holding their cloaks aloft. On the opposite bank, a large silver-backed wolf slunk out from the shadow of the trees and bared its teeth at the advancing ships beneath.

Suddenly there was a mighty shout that echoed over the river and startled the black birds which flew off low over the water. The sailors, so close now that she could see their bearded faces, seized their oars, hitting the water in short rapid strokes that stirred the river up into a milky foam. They were steering straight for shore, heading directly for the bank beneath her.

Ellie cried out and turned back into the room. At that moment the Guildhall clock began to ring, its chimes welcome and familiar. From far off she heard the hum of the army helicopter as it set off on its early morning patrol over the city. The wind had started up again, pelting the window pane with large raindrops. She looked down towards the river-bank again. There were no strange ships. The Foyle snaked blackly past the sleeping city with its familiar landmarks, both old and new. There was the slender spire of the cathedral, there the green dome of the department store in The Diamond, and there the massive swaying arms of a crane rising above a building site on the quays.

What is happening to me? Was I sleep-walking? Did I dream those ships? Baffled and a bit frightened, Ellie sat down on the edge of her bed, trying to steady her breath which came in short painful gasps. A voice – a voice which might have been Harald's – was echoing in her ears. *Beware the curse of Fenri*, it said. She repeated the phrase aloud, trying to make sense of it. Who or what was Fenri? What did it mean? Had she just imagined the ghostly figure at the window, the phantom fleet of Viking warriors? Or had she truly seen a ghost?

She lay back against the pillow. Her head ached and her limbs felt exhausted as if she had been running all night long but she fought the waves of tiredness that flowed over her. She would not allow herself to sleep again. With eyes stretched wide, she stared at the ceiling above her bed, fighting back the images of the strange world of the foreign sailors. You are in your own room, safe and secure, she told herself. Nothing bad can happen here. She repeated the phrases to herself, as if the saying of them might be enough to make them true. A loose corner of peeling wallpaper flapped in the draught from the window. The water tank suddenly juddered and gurgled. A car sped past the house, its headlamps briefly illuminating the room. This is normal, she thought, this is the real world – it was just a dream I had, nothing but a dream. Above her head, the cracks in the plaster of the old ceiling seemed to roll and shift, flowing like vast continental rivers towards the central light bulb, throwing out tributaries which snaked down the sides of the dormer window. Immediately the picture of Harald and his ghost-ships gliding up the Foyle reappeared and she shuddered. She felt possessed, as if someone had crept beneath her skin, manufacturing her dreams, compelling her to watch them.

Chapter 2

This is the shipping forecast. There are gale warnings
for Viking, Fair Isle, Faeroes, South East Iceland, Bailey,
Hebrides, Rockall, Malin.

All that day the rain sheeted down. Torrents of rain
rushed noisily along the gutters of the city streets until
the drains gave out and overflowed. With nowhere else
to go, the waters advanced into people's gardens,
seeped into the ground floors of shoe shops and cafés
and trickled over the threshold of public houses. Ellie's
house, perched high up on one of the hills above the
city, was in no danger of flooding. From her bedroom
window in the attic she watched the swollen river rise.
Sometime in the middle of the afternoon – no-one could
have pinpointed the exact moment – it overflowed its
banks. Water swirled into the railway station on the one
side, and lapped the front door of city shops and offices
on the other. Parked cars were tossed up onto the
pavements and into front gardens where they lay like
abandoned outsize toys. All day long the sirens of police
cars and fire engines wailed and screamed along the
quays and over the bridge while the storm grew louder

and more threatening. The city grew dark under the shadow of black thunder clouds. Lightning ripped across the sky.

Even indoors, there was no escaping the menace of the storm. The house itself seemed to grow gloomy and unfamiliar, as if possessed by clumsy ghosts. Doors in upstairs rooms slammed shut of their own volition. Curtains unexpectedly swelled and billowed out, and draughts whistled under doors, lifting the corners of rugs, rattling the cups drying on the draining-board. At every window, the panes shook themselves loose and set up a mighty rattling and juddering.

Alone in the house, and feeling cold and exhausted from her disturbed sleep the night before, Ellie took herself off to her room in the early afternoon and threw herself on the bed. Hennessy, her ginger cat, followed her, mewing indignantly at the noise raging outside, and climbed on to her bed. When she made no attempt to push him away, he settled down like a plump warm cushion on her back and fell asleep. Lulled by his breathing, Ellie let herself relax. Her eyelids drooped.

She had been asleep no more than a few seconds when suddenly there was an enormous clap of thunder. The wind howled and the sky which had grown dark as night was lit up by a streak of silver forked lightning. Ellie sat bolt upright just as the water broke over her in a churning boiling inferno. She fought for breath and struck out against the waves which dragged her down into their cold watery grasp, mauling and clawing at her limbs, then tossing her up into the air again. She could taste the salt in her mouth and feel the tangled ropes of seaweed catching at her legs, knotting themselves around her. So this is drowning, thought Ellie, almost with resignation. Another long burst of thunder rolled across the sky and the world exploded in a frenzy of lightning. A voice within her prayed, *Give me strength, O Thor, and deliver me from your anger.*

Ellie struck out again, this time determined to save herself. Her arm knocked against something hard.

"Ouch," she shouted out and opened her eyes. She looked around, baffled by the ordinariness of everything before her. She was in her room, high and dry above the city. Beside her, on the floor, lay her bedside table lamp, its ceramic base broken clean in two. Her knuckles were bleeding.

The sun was streaming into the room directly onto her pillow so that she was almost blinded by the light. The storm, it seemed, was over. Somewhat shakily, for the dream and the sensation of drowning were still very clear to her, she stood up and walked across to the dressing-table where Hennessy the cat was lying in front of the mirror. From downstairs in the kitchen came the clatter of cups and the murmur of the television. At least she was no longer alone, she realised with relief. Her parents were back from work.

"Come on Hennessy," she murmured, reaching out to scratch his ear. "Time for supper."

The cat, responding to the tone of her voice, arched its back and stretched. As Ellie moved forward to lift him into her arms, she glanced at the mirror to lift a strand of hair from her forehead. Behind her reflection, stood another figure, its head bowed, its fair hair falling in wet tendrils across its face. She turned in alarm to look over her shoulder but there was no-one in the room – and when she turned to face the mirror again, only her own reflection stared back at her, open-mouthed, and pale with fear. She seized the cat in her arms and fled from the room.

Downstairs, both her parents were standing in the middle of the living-room, watching the television screen. As Ellie entered, her father held up a hand for silence. Like everybody else in Northern Ireland, her parents were obsessed with the news, always half expecting to hear that someone they knew had been murdered or that a bomb had ripped apart another town. Recently they were even jumpier. Ellie picked up the newspaper and turned to the TV listings. With any luck there would be a film or something watchable on so that she wouldn't have to go to bed until really late. If she could only persuade her parents to go up first, she might even sleep on the sofa. There was something spooky about her own room now, something that made her feel both excited and scared at the same time.

The newsreader's voice droned on about the widespread disruption to services and public transport after the second day of severe weather conditions in the North-West.

"Several boats were torn from their moorings along the north coast, and on Lough Foyle an off-shore trawler has run aground after it attempted to shelter from the storm on the high seas . . . Early reports suggest a fire may have broken out in the engine-room of the ship but we understand there are no casualties among the crew members . . . we go over to Charles McFadden live from the scene in Donegal . . . Charles . . . "

Shocked, Ellie looked up from the newspaper and stared at the screen. The reporter was speaking from a helicopter hovering above the beach where the trawler had gone aground. *The* beach. What with the noise of the engines and the howling winds, it was difficult to make out exactly what he was saying but Ellie didn't need to hear a word. She stared open-mouthed at the screen, at the incoming tide throwing itself against the ship which lay on its side near the water's edge. Beyond that she saw the sea, angry and steel-grey except where it was whipped into charging white horses.

There was no doubt about it. It was the beach in her dream. The long windswept strand and the cliff and the dunes were just the same. And the dark hulk of the shipwreck. She could almost smell the salt on the wind and hear the creaking of the smouldering timbers.

"Have we ever been there, Mum?" she asked, in as casual a tone as she could muster.

"For God's sake, Ellie, what would you have been doing down there? It's across the border."

"It's near here though, isn't it?" Ellie persisted.

"I suppose it is." Her mother agreed, reluctantly. "The other side of Lough Foyle."

The television camera tracked over the beach, giving her the same bird's eye view that she had had in her dream. The reporter's voice crackled and spat, carried off out to sea by the roaring wind. Ellie sat transfixed, wondering desperately what to do next. Was the storm her fault? Had she somehow made the shipwreck happen? She tried to recall the other dreams she had been having, fearful that she was about to unleash a series of catastrophes upon the country.

"All eight men on board have been rescued," concluded the newsreader "and taken to hospital in Londonderry. We'll have an update on the fate of the *Viking Warrior* and other stories in the nine o'clock news."

As the captions rolled, they showed again the film of

the trawler lying on its side with the sea churning and tossing all around it. The *Viking Warrior*, the man had said. Ellie shuddered. Dreaming about a shipwreck on that very beach was bad enough – a beach she had never been on – but the weirdest coincidence was the name of the ship: the *Viking Warrior*. Weren't those Viking ships she had seen, that phantom fleet coming up the river from the sea? What could it mean? Was there something she should have done when the dreams first started weeks ago? Someone she should have warned? She felt herself redden with guilt as if she had been caught in the act of some crime, as if somehow she was responsible for what had happened.

She looked across the room at her parents' faces. Her dad, still standing in front of the TV, was engrossed in the sports round-up. Her mother had thrown off her shoes and was stretched out on the sofa, doing the crossword.

"I've had this dream," began Ellie.

"Mmmm," said her mother absent-mindedly without even looking up from the paper.

"I only wish I had had a nap myself. With that racket last night I didn't get a wink of sleep," said her father, picking up his briefcase and drifting out of the room. "I just lay there thinking how I was going to pay for it if the roof blew off the house."

There was no point in telling them about it, Ellie thought. Even if they did listen, they'd think she was making it all up or they'd just shrug and say it was a coincidence. Perhaps it was. But all the same, it made her flesh crawl.

All evening she went through the motions of having supper and chatting and watching television even as her mind raced with thoughts of the boat blazing on the beach and the fleet of ghost-ships on the river. Mostly she thought of the man with the ghostly wet face that she had seen reflected in her bedroom mirror. She wanted to tell someone but knew they would just make fun of her. "Take a hike, Ellie, with all your yarns. There's no such thing as ghosts or bogey men," she could imagine her father saying. At ten o'clock, she could stand it no longer and reluctantly dragged herself upstairs. On the landing, she stopped to look down on the river, still full and grey and swollen. In her mind's eye, she saw the monstrous fleet of ghost ships, advancing in single file around the curve of the river bank, the wind howling in their sails. Viking ships? Viking warriors? She glanced down river beyond the round blue hills that rose behind the city. Over the horizon the river broadened out and entered the lough. Beyond that was the sea and the beach where the real *Viking Warrior* had gone aground.

"I'll go tomorrow," she said aloud.

Only you will know where to look, said the voice in her head.

"I'll find you," she replied.

It was only later that she realised she had been speaking to Harald.

Chapter 3

Water crashes against the coast, wearing and cracking
the rocks. Air becomes trapped and compressed in rock
cracks as each wave crashes against the coast. As the
waves move back, the compressed air expands quickly,
causing tiny explosions which eventually shatter the
rock. Stones and sand are hurled against the coast by the
waves. These help break down the coast.

New Complete Geography 1, Charles Hayes

The following morning, as soon as her parents were
safely out of the way, Ellie took her bike out of the
garage and set off alone out of the city. She cycled slowly
across the bridge, stopping once to lean over the railings
and look at the river. The water was still so high it
slapped against the lower deck of the bridge which had
been closed off to traffic. Even in the city streets, water
still eddied and swirled around blocked drains. Tattered
sheets of newspapers flapped across the streets and
occasionally she had to veer around broken branches and
fallen sections of advertising hoarding. The city after the
storm looked as if a bomb had hit it. Getting away, even
for a day, suddenly seemed like a wonderful idea.

A line of personnel carriers and a tank signalled her arrival at the border between Northern Ireland and the Republic. The customs shed, a huge ugly pre-fab, once painted in camouflage colours, stood empty and neglected behind barbed wire, burnt out in some forgotten bombing incident. Traffic had slowed to a crawl as the cars bumped over the ramps across the road. A distracted soldier waved Ellie past.

WELCOME TO DONEGAL, said a notice.

And that was it. She had crossed the border. Ever since she could remember, her life had been overshadowed by that border, and then, when you came to it, there was nothing there, it was just an invisible line on a map. As she rode along – quite quickly for the trip to see the shipwreck was going to take all day – she looked at the small fields, the low farm-houses with their smoking chimneys, the piles of muddy rain-soaked leaves blown under the hedges. Looking back, you couldn't say what lay on 'her' side of the border or what was on the other side. But you couldn't say it didn't matter. There were all sorts of invisible lines out there, lines that people found it difficult to cross for fear of what they would find on the other side.

The wind whistled, cold and sharp, around her ears and she heard the echoing voice, *Only you will know where to find me*. Brusquely, she shunted her bike into a higher gear and rode on, trying hard to shake off the ghostly image of the blond boy-man at her bedroom window the previous night.

At length she reached the village nearest to the scene of the disaster. It was a small unimpressive little place, with one long street which sprawled untidily up a hill, its back to the sea, but now in its moment of fame, it was hopping with visitors. There were newsmen and photographers hung about with cameras and microphones milling around the post office; there were police cars parked outside the hotel and groups of sightseers wielding binoculars and telescopes striding like moon-walkers in their bulky anoraks and wellington boots into the public bar. A couple of playful brown dogs, unused to all this commotion on their territory, ran alongside Ellie's bike, barking excitedly at her heels.

"Get off," she snarled at them but they followed her anyway.

She could smell the tang of the sea, could smell the sand and the salt and the seaweed and she could hear the low roar of the ocean rolling up on to the beach like an untamed beast. Between the houses, she caught tantalising glimpses of sand and cliff but there never seemed to be any right of way down to the strand. She cycled faster up the hill, heart thumping, imagining that someone was leading her on, calling her forward.

The last house at the top of the hill was a long low cottage, set back off the street, with two petrol pumps on the forecourt. A rusty sign advertising engine oil swung above the front door and Ellie could just pick out the name MATTHEW MCLOUGHLIN, PROPRIETOR written in faded black letters across the front of the house. She jumped off her bike and steered it around the gable end to the back yard.

The yard was cluttered with all manner of flotsam and jetsam. There were old rusting barrels and buoys scattered amid heaps of lobster pots and tangles of old tar-stained ropes which someone had dragged up from the shoreline. A huge stack of bald tyres leant up against a wall, rotting in the salt-laden air. Ellie laid her bike against it and ran towards the crumbling dry stone wall at the back of the yard.

It was then she had her first clear view of the sea and the shipwreck. The strand lay beneath her, curving around the bay in a wide open semi-circle backed by sand dunes, and ended in a sheer dramatic headland opposite. The *Viking Warrior* lay on its side at the bottom of the cliff-face. It was a terrible-looking old tub, so rusty and vulnerable she couldn't imagine it ever being safe out on the open sea. It was no wonder it had got into trouble.

Ellie jumped off the wall and began to run down the path to the beach. It was rough and stony with two deep ruts running along the sides and a thick belt of wiry grass growing down the centre, clearly unused by anyone for a very long time and yet somehow familiar to her. Every part of it was familiar.

It *was* the beach she had dreamt of. Only something jarred, something she could not put her finger on. One part of the picture was not right. She scanned the beach, trying to blot out the distracting commotion beneath and summon up exactly how it had appeared to her in her dreams. And it *was* a hive of activity – men in hard hats were directing a pair of huge yellow mechanical diggers across the sand above the tide-line; others were standing on the deck-rails of the trawler gesticulating and shouting to the men standing in the water beneath the ship. Offshore, between the strand and the tiny whale-backed island which lay outside the bay, a fleet of small boats bobbed about on the waves while another larger trawler lay at anchor in the channel, possibly intending to refloat the wreck, Ellie thought.

She broke into a clumsy run, her feet sinking in the

soft wet expanse of sand. Above her a large yellow helicopter droned and whirred, its rotating blades flattening the wiry marram grass as it passed over her. The dark shadow it cast crawled across the beach like a monstrous crab until the helicopter dropped height to come in over the cliff to land.

Ellie watched it hover and slowly come to rest high above her on the headland. A lone figure was standing by the edge, staring out to sea. A tall slender man whose blond hair was whipped back off his face by the draught from the whirring helicopter blades. The sight of him triggered some memory in Ellie's brain, something too fleeting to grasp. For an instant she felt as if she had just witnessed something of great importance, as if a snapshot had been passed quickly in front of her eyes without having enough time to understand what image it held. The helicopter, perched high on the edge of the cliff, shimmered and appeared to dissolve, disappearing in the swirling mist that seemed suddenly to roll in off the sea. In its place stood the shadowy outline of another ship, a smaller, flatter ship than the one that lay abandoned on the seashore.

Come and find me, said a familiar voice in her head.

Ellie stopped running and put her hands over her ears. It's just the sound of the wind, she thought, but the voice would not be silent. She breathed in deeply, but almost gagged as a plume of thick black smoke caught the back of her throat – smoke which drifted down over the strand from the blazing ship of her dreams, a ship alight up on the cliff. She could feel the heat of the flames as they leapt up towards the black evening sky.

Only of course it was not night at all. And there was

no blazing ship high up on the headland. Only the two mechanical diggers trundling across the strand ahead of her, the seagulls wheeling and screaming overhead and a policeman howling against the wind into the radio on his collar. Why then did she smell burning and hear the warriors drumming their sticks on their wooden shields? Why then did she feel that if she dared raise her eyes and look up on the cliff the figure of Harald would be standing there, staring out to sea?

A squally shower had started up. Ellie darted across the sand to shelter among the boulders at the foot of the cliff. The wind tossed her long hair into a tangled stream behind her. It was easy to imagine this same wind battering the coast since time began, whipping the sea into a frenzy of froth and foam, tearing at the roots of the grasses, and even sweeping a ship off the high seas and hurling it up on to the shore.

But not up on top of a cliff, she thought. In the dream, the ship was up on the headland. Hunched behind a large rock, Ellie peered out at the battered old trawler and the incoming tide swirling around its base. That's not the ship I dreamt about, she realised. It was another, a real Viking ship that I saw. And the fire was no accident. They had set it alight deliberately.

She stepped out from behind the boulders and looked about her. The white sand was strewn with tangled heaps of bright glistening seaweed thrown up along the tide line but at the foot of the cliff itself lay a huge mound of dark brown earth and rock. Grass still clung to some of the larger boulders. There were even clumps of pink flowers. She walked slowly around one of the large rocks. The body of a sheep, its neck cruelly twisted and a dark stain that was probably blood spreading across its shoulder, was lying on its back behind the boulder. Ellie backed away in disgust. How did that get there, she wondered.

Her eyes moved to the jagged face of the cliff. "These rocks shouldn't be here," she said slowly, as the pictures from her dreams grew clearer, "the storm last night must have made part of the cliff collapse. The sheep must have fallen down when the land gave way."

As she spoke, an enormous wave struck the rocks behind her with a loud crash. She wheeled around, her nerves in tatters, but a sneaky gully of icy water had already lapped over her shoes.

"Damn, damn, damn," she swore, jumping back. As she did so, the water turned and was sucked down in a little eddy under the nearest boulder. As it ebbed away, a short ivory-coloured object poked up from under the rock as if a hidden hand was offering it to her. Ellie knelt down and touched it. It came away from the wet sand with a satisfying gulp . . . She rubbed the sand off it and stooped to rinse it in a pool of water beneath one of the rocks. It was a slender arc-shaped thing, about six inches long and a dull creamy colour. I should know what this is, thought Ellie, running the tips of her fingers along the indentations on one side of the arc. Then another thought struck her, or maybe it was the same voice which had spoken to her earlier, *You were meant to find this, Ellie. It is part of the haunting. You must listen to your dreams. Now find me.*

She stroked the strange object and laid it against her cheek to feel its smoothness. It didn't feel like a shell or a stone. As she drew it down her cheek, pushing aside strands of her wet tangled hair, she had the sensation that someone, someone who had lived long before her, had often done the same thing.

No, no, she thought angrily. There's nothing here but a clapped-out old ship that should never have been allowed to sail on the open seas. My dreams were just that, dreams. I don't know what I'm doing here. And now I'm going to have to cycle all the way home again in the rain.

She thrust the thing she had picked up into her pocket and dashed out from behind the shelter of the boulders, breaking into a run and turning away her face as she passed the trawler as if ashamed to pay it any more attention. The salvage men shouted as they hauled on their ropes, their voices drifting in and out of earshot. The rain was getting heavier by the minute and the sea turning mean and choppy. She should never have come. At least nobody knew what an idiot she had been, coming all this way just because of a dream.

Angry at her own gullibility, and determined now to get home as fast as possible, she ran back across the strand, never once looking back until she reached the wall behind the old garage. She quickly clambered over the loose stones and, with hands so cold they were curled up like claws, she started to unlock her bicycle chain.

"And who might you be, then, making yourself at home on my premises?"

Ellie wheeled around in alarm. An old man came striding towards her. He was tall and wiry, though a little bit stooped. He wore a woolly fisherman's cap, pulled low down over his ears. His cheeks were marbled with broken red veins. Ellie gulped and bit her lip.

"I'm sorry. I didn't think anyone lived here," she

stammered. "I'm going now."

"You should be safe in your own home," the old man went on as he came nearer. "It's no weather for playing on the strand. It was a wild night here last night and the wind is rising again. There'll be no Viking ships coming into the lough tonight."

Ellie turned to him sharply. "What did you say?"

"Just my little joke. That old trawler is called the *Viking Warrior*. Did you never hear the old poem written by one of the ancient scribes about the Vikings –

Do not fret for me for tonight my heart's at ease
The harsh Northmen only set out on tranquil seas.

The man who wrote that poem all those hundreds of years ago knew the Vikings wouldn't come to plunder on a stormy night."

"Did any Vikings really land here? In the old days, I mean," asked Ellie. She had never heard of Vikings in Northern Ireland.

"Aye surely," said the man, picking his way carefully though the rusting hulks of old tractors to come and stand beside her. "There were fleets of them all along these coasts, coming up the rivers and into the loughs, pillaging and laying waste to all before them."

"I thought they were only in Dublin and York and big places like that."

The old man smiled. "You know what my name is? McLoughlin."

"Oh," said Ellie, "that's my name too."

"Well, that doesn't surprise me. I've heard it's one of the most common names in Derry. But do you know what McLoughlin means?"

Ellie shook her head.

"Son of the Viking, that's what it means if you translate it from the Irish – so don't tell me there were no Vikings around here. You can't have sons of Vikings without there being Vikings around about. And another thing that makes me think there must have been Vikings living in these parts – there was a type of boat that was common around here that you didn't find anywhere else in Ireland and it looked just like an old Viking ship, rounded at the bow and the stern and with one big square brown sail. We called them dromtheims – the schoolmaster long ago told me once that they were called after Trondheim. That's a place in Norway, where the Vikings came from."

He turned his face to hers and held her gaze. His pupils, green and flecked with yellow like a cat's eyes, shone at her from watery red rims: ageless eyes, she thought, in an old man's face. She shifted uncomfortably and knelt down to secure the bicycle chain on the bars. As she did so, the thing she had found on the beach slipped out of her pocket.

"What's that you have there?" said the old man.

Ellie bent down to pick it up but Mr McLoughlin gestured for her to hand it to him.

"I picked it up on the beach," she said, "it's nothing – just an old fishbone probably – but it's pretty."

"No, it's not from a fish," said Mr McLoughlin, running his fingers down the strange teeth-like marks along its length. "It doesn't even look like something that's been in the sea for any length of time. Where did you find it?"

Ellie jealously put her hand out to take it back from him. Her eyes flickered towards the boulders on the far side of the strand under the cliff but she didn't reply.

"You're not local, are you?" the old man continued.

Ellie shook her head.

"This has always been a great place for beachcombers. It would astonish you the things that get washed up here off ships." He seemed to be studying her intently, watching her put away the key of the padlock in her jeans pocket. "Would you like to come in and wait for the rain to ease off a bit before you get on your way. You could have a cup of tea."

Ellie hesitated. It was very wet. A hot drink would be great before the long cycle back home. But you weren't supposed to accept invitations like that from strangers, even from someone as harmless-looking as Mr McLoughlin.

The old man put out his hand and smiled, showing a mouthful of perfectly even false teeth. "Sure, you've no cause to worry about me. Matt's the name. Matt Mc Loughlin, like I said. God knows, we're probably related if you go back far enough. Come into the house a wee minute – I have something I found down on the strand this morning that might be of interest to a young explorer like yourself."

Ellie followed Mr McLoughlin through the back door of the house and into a large stone-flagged kitchen where a kettle was already whistling on an old black range. The old man walked over to the high mantelpiece above it and rummaged about among all the flotsam and jetsam he kept there – dried starfish, a big coiled shell of the kind you put your ear to to listen to the roar of the ocean, pieces of driftwood that had been twisted and sculpted by the sea into fantastic shapes.

"There we are, I knew I had left it up here somewhere." He smiled at her the way adults do when they know they're giving someone a surprise and pressed into her hand something small and round and cold, closing her fingers over it.

Ellie opened her hand. On her palm lay a tiny irregularly-shaped silver coin on which you could just make out the head of a man and some strange lettering around the edge.

"I had a mind to send it off to Dublin," said Mr Mc Loughlin, "to the museum maybe, to find out where it came from but you can hang on to it. Maybe you can find out how old it is."

"Where did you get it?" asked Ellie softly.

"I found it, this morning, down by yonder boulders," said Mr McLoughlin, pointing out his window at the boulders on the far side of the strand. "Another big chunk of the headland fell down last night with a bang that would have woken the dead . . . I heard it even above the storm."

A cold shiver ran down Ellie's spine as if someone had stepped on her grave.

"That's where I found this thing too," said Ellie while another voice in her head whispered softly, *Only you will know where to find me.*

Chapter 4

"I seemed to move among a world of ghosts
And feel myself the shadow of a dream."
The Princess, Prologue, Alfred Lord Tennyson

As Ellie wheeled her bike out from behind Matt Mc
Loughlin's garage and took off down the main street of
the village, night was already falling, even though it was
just after four o'clock, for the clocks had been turned
back that very weekend. The rain had eased off a little
but a mist was rolling in from the sea, blurring the
outlines of the houses and enveloping the countryside
in a melancholy damp shroud. Disheartened by the
length of the journey ahead of her, Ellie bent her head
against the rain and concentrated on nothing but the
steady turning of the wheels. Shortly after leaving the
village and the lights of the houses behind her, the road
became bumpier, as if pockmarked by pot-holes, but
conscious only of the growing darkness and the
thickening fog, Ellie at first didn't notice. It was only
when the shadowy forms of half a dozen sheep loomed
up in front of her that she realised she had come off the
main road and was riding along a rutted untarred path.

No car had passed by her for some time. She wheeled slowly to a stop and dismounted. All around her was darkness and silence, silence but for the low rumble of the sea and the occasional bleating of the sheep. Desperately seeking some landmark that would tell her where she had got to, she turned slowly around.

Far off, she could make out the lights of the village, strung out along the road like a line of dim Christmas decorations. With mounting horror, she realised she had accidentally taken a left fork and had circled around the bay in the direction of the cliffs – when she should have carried on straight along the main road, heading for the border and home. She must be up on top of the headland, overlooking the strand.

"No, no, no," she shouted angrily into the wind at the prospect of retracing her journey so far. Now it would take even longer to get home. Furious, she made to mount the bike again when suddenly there was a resounding crash as the sea hit the rocks. A massive wave leapt skyward, scattering heavy drops of spray all over her.

I must be right at the very edge, she thought nervously, remembering the sheer drop to the beach below. In the near darkness she could hear a tearing ripping sound. Behind her the small huddle of sheep bleated piteously and ran off. A large rabbit, or it might have been a hare, bolted out from a hole beside the path and passed inches in front of her as it raced off inland across the bog.

There was a low rumble which grew louder. Another wave, even bigger than before, struck the cliff. The earth beneath her feet trembled as the water broke over it. Ellie seized the handlebars of her bike and started to run back inland, away from the edge of the cliff. She had hardly gone twenty yards when the ground seemed to groan in agony. With an almighty wrench, a section of the earth behind her gave way and fell in slow motion towards the strand beneath. Ellie felt herself hurtling through space as if someone had grabbed her by the shoulders and was dragging her further back from the cliff edge. She lay face down on the boggy earth where she had fallen, her hands covering her head, not daring to move a muscle. Gradually the rumble of falling stones and earth ceased. The wind sighed. Even the sea grew calm as if it had exhausted its fury in destroying the cliff face.

Ellie sat up and rubbed her hands nervously over her arms and legs to check if she had been hurt but apart from a graze on her cheek, she seemed all right. She began to move cautiously back to the path, creeping on all fours so that she could feel her way forward, afraid that the next step might be her last. The ground was pitted with holes and ruts, as if it were just a matter of time before the whole place gave up the struggle and fell away into the sea.

"Please, get me out of here," she prayed, cowering as another huge wave struck the headland. "Don't let any more land fall away."

She peered anxiously into the night, hoping to see the dark shape of her bike ahead of her or brush against its cold metal, but it had gone, carried off in the landslide into the churning sea beneath, she imagined. There was no choice but to walk back all the way to the village and phone her parents. In any case, they would already be home from work and worried that she was not there. Despondently, she abandoned her search for the bike and stood up.

Directly ahead of her stood a lop-sided post with a life-belt tied to it. Then out of the darkness, an eerie green rectangular shape about four feet long began to form. It hovered at the very edge of the cliff. Ellie stopped dead in her tracks and squinted at it. Whatever it was was throwing off a dull pulsating glow.

"Is anybody there?" she called out, interrogating the dark even though she knew there would be no reply. The voice from her dreams began to echo in her head. *Only you will know where to find me*, it said in that sad plaintive voice, and as she looked on, transfixed, the doubled-over figure of a man unfolded itself and floated up from the eerie green rectangle to stand in front of her bathed in a faint, almost transparent, light as if lit by an internal torch.

Ellie recognised the long slim face of Harald, the man whose life was haunting her dreams, the same man whose image she had already seen that afternoon, she now realised, for it was Harald that she had seen standing on the edge of the cliff as the helicopter came in to land.

She felt no fear, only a deep sense of sadness, and curiosity, as she watched him. At first his features appeared young, vital. Then his head seemed to be wrenched back violently. His face gradually aged, growing old beyond measure as the flesh fell away from him. His skin became taut and drawn, stretched so tightly over the bones that she could see the skull becoming visible beneath the face. Within moments the image had faded. The green transparent light dimmed and vanished.

"He died here," she said, half to herself, but the inner voice corrected her – no, he was *murdered* here.

For another moment, she stood motionless, uncertain of what she had seen, trying to dismiss it as a trick of the light and the shock she had had when the cliff had fallen away. There are no such things as ghosts, she repeated to herself over and over, denying the very thing she had just seen, while another part of her longed for the figure to come back, to come back and speak to her, to tell her what he wanted of her.

The rain had eased off again so that now it was easier to see where she was. She began to trudge back along the coastal path, listening to the rain splashing in secret boggy pools and the nearby tow of the sea dragging stones up and down the beach. She imagined the same waves on their journey southwards from the Faeroes and the Norwegian sea, swelling and roaring in through the narrow mouths of Lough Foyle and Lough Swilly like a wild untamed monster. She fancied she could smell on the wind's breath the chill of ice-capped mountains and the icebergs of the northern ocean. Men like the ones she had seen in her dreams had set out across those empty oceans a thousand years ago. They had never seemed very real to her before, not like actual people who had walked on the same hills and beaches as her, men and women who had felt cold or hungry or sad or tired. They were just history. But Harald was no longer history. His long slim face was becoming as real to her as her own. She had the curious sensation that as she walked towards the village lights, he was watching her, watching over her.

And all at once, she felt all the people who had ever lived crowd in around her, and march in procession with her – not just the recent dead, people like her own grandparents or the victims of the bombings and killings of the North that she heard about on the news each evening, but the ancient dead. Behind her she felt hordes of them rise up and walk beside her, ancient warring chieftains, Viking sailors, Norman soldiers and castle-builders, the planters who had come from Scotland with the promise of land, the emaciated figures of victims of the famine, drowned fishermen and consumptive babies. Nothing on earth remained of these people from long ago. No-one was left to tell their story but Ellie recognised them, every one, and heard far off their distant voices. She had never seen a dead person before, unless you counted some dusty skeletons in a museum, their long thin bones huddled in old passage-graves, or mummified Egyptians in brightly-coloured coffins. Now it seemed as if layer after layer of them were rising up from the earth where they had been laid down like strata of rock, one on top of the other, exposing deeper and deeper veins until Harald's age could seep out on to the surface and meet hers. Why had he brought her to this lonely place, she wondered. What was so important that he had invaded her life, her dreams? And why had he chosen her? Her hand reached instinctively for the smooth white arc in her pocket and stroked it protectively.

Chapter 5

" . . . it was laid out for a person from the time the crown of his head came into the world where his sod of death was. For this person it was laid out that for him or for her, the side of the road would be as a sod of death, for another the middle of the field, or out on the brown mountain or in the lonelinesss of the wood, or – God save us from the danger! – a person could have as sod of death a violent death."

Medieval Irish Lyrics

"It's a pity about your bike but it was a mercy you didn't lose your life," said Matt McLoughlin thoughtfully when Ellie had finished telling him how she had strayed off the road and how some more of the cliff had fallen away into the sea. "For all the danger you were in, your sod of death was not up on that headland."

"What does that mean?" asked Ellie sharply. She was sitting by the range in the old man's house waiting for her parents to arrive and take her home. If the sound of her mother's voice was anything to go by, Ellie knew she was in for a row. They were more upset that she had gone off without telling them than about her nearly being killed.

"Did you never hear tell of the sod of death?" asked Mr McLoughlin. "In the old days, they used to say each of us had our own sod of death, the place where death would meet us as soon as we put our foot on it. All it means I suppose, is that when the time comes for us to die, we can't avoid our destiny. Do you take sugar in your tea?" he went on, pushing a mug across the table towards her.

"Do you believe that, Mr McLoughlin?" Ellie asked after a couple of minutes. She had been so close to death up there on the headland, closer than she had ever been before. A couple of metres would have made all the difference. Perhaps that was why her brain had conjured up the image of Harald. She hadn't seen a ghost. She had been suffering from shock, that was all. Visibility was terrible anyway, she rationalised. In the bright warm kitchen, the idea of ghosts seemed ridiculous.

"About the sod of death?" she prompted. "Do you really believe there's such a thing?"

"Aye indeed I do. It's like that cat there," he said, pointing to an old battle-scarred cat sleeping at the foot of the range. "He has his nine lives but one of these days he'll put his foot wrong and that'll be that. Did you see the story in the papers a while ago about the cow that fell off that cliff back in the summer? She was just grazing quietly up there on the cliff when the ground gave away beneath her. Well, that was that, we all thought, including the man that owned the cow. But five days later, wasn't I sitting out there on the old iron seat in the yard behind and didn't the cow come swimming on to the strand and wander up the beach, bellowing fit to burst."

"And she was all right?" asked Ellie, unsure if he was pulling her leg.

"Aye surely, not a bit the worse for her adventure. No, it's a known fact, every creature has its sod of death, and we stay in the land of the living until we set our foot on it."

"I saw a dead sheep on the beach this afternoon. I think it must have fallen off the cliff too," said Ellie.

"I'm telling you, that cliff is a mighty dangerous place for man and beast at the moment. You should steer well clear of it. There's a caravan park just a bit further on where a couple of young families are still living – hippies I suppose you'd call them. I've warned them to be on their way but there's no talking to them. They think I'm joking but, mark my words, we'll lose a lot more of that cliff before the winter's out."

Mr McLoughlin lifted the teapot to refill their cups. His hands shook with the weight of the pot. Ellie watched the prominent blue veins on the backs of his hands, like blue worms beneath his skin, and wondered how old he was. As if he knew what she must be thinking, Mr McLoughlin gave a half sort of laugh and said, "There's nothing much to be said for growing old, is there? A man can live too long."

Embarrassed, Ellie shook her head but the old man went on. "I have my plot all bought and paid for. The sod of burial holds no fear for me."

"What do you mean, your sod of burial?"

"That's what they call the place where a body is meant to be buried and rest until judgement day – unless of course his grave has been disturbed. There's nothing more evil than vandalising another man's grave. You'd never know what kind of curse would be on someone who did a thing like that."

Ellie shuddered and sipped her tea. She was exhausted and wanted nothing more than to be back in her own home. She hoped her parents would arrive soon – even though they were certain to give her a really hard time, and not just for making them come all this way to fetch her. She could hear her mother's voice already, going on about how people like them didn't cross the border. And then there was the bike. Her father would make his usual speech about money not growing on trees. As if losing it hurt them more than it did her. What was she going to do without a bike? She stared down at the irregularly-shaped stone flags of the kitchen floor, feeling pretty sorry for herself.

The stones swam in front of her eyes, moving and shifting into weird patterns, settling into a long oval shape which somehow reminded her of a ship. Images from her dreams came back to her, of the men beating their wooden shields, of the women wailing up on the headland around the blazing ship. What is happening to me, she thought. Perhaps I am going mad. That's what happens to people, they start hearing voices in their head and seeing visions. She sat up sharply and looked around the room, afraid suddenly that she had fallen asleep at the table and had said something out loud. Get a grip, Ellie, she told herself crossly. The old man had moved to an armchair by the side of the range, the cat lying languidly across his feet.

"How old is this house, Mr McLoughlin?" she asked him.

"It's a fair age," he replied. "Why do you ask?"

"This floor here looks like it's made of real stones, not tiles."

"Well, you're right about that. I remember when I was a child, six or seven years old maybe, seeing my grandfather carting rocks up from the strand to lay that floor when he started building this part of the house close on seventy years ago. The rest of the house is newer. Over the years, we all sort of built on bits as we needed them, for the garage and the shop."

"So those stones came up from the beach?"

"Aye," the old man agreed. "They're a fair age, those same stones."

"Do you believe in ghosts, Mr McLoughlin?"

Mr McLoughlin leant forward and looked straight at Ellie, holding his gaze steady.

"What put that idea into your head? Have you seen one?"

Ellie looked away, blushing. "No," she said, "I just thought you might know stories about ghosts, around here. It's the sort of lonely place you'd expect to find them," she blundered on, too embarrassed to admit to what she had seen earlier on the headland. It all seemed crazy now.

"Well," said the old man, "I'd say the earth is haunted but maybe not in the way people mean when they talk of ghosts, of walkers after death. Often I have the sense that there are other unseen presences following us around, watching us, all the generations that went before us."

Ellie shivered involuntarily. That was exactly what she had thought walking back from the cliff when she felt as if she was under the protection of all those ancient ghosts. The cat slowly uncurled itself from Mr McLoughlin's feet, yawned, stretched the full length of its body and padded towards the door.

"Cats don't like talk of ghosts," said Mr McLoughlin. "Will you open that door for him?"

"Do you think a man might come back to haunt the place where he died? To his sod of death?" asked Ellie. A swirl of cold air rushed into the room as the cat left.

"Well, I have no way of telling you if that happens or not for I have never witnessed such a thing myself, thanks be to God," replied the old man, "but there are so many accounts of such things I wouldn't deny it. There are restless ghosts, people who have a score to settle or some business left undone. I'd say a man might have to walk again."

As he spoke, a car door slammed out on the road, then another. Thank God her parents had arrived, thought Ellie. Even though they were probably going to murder her.

The journey home was tense. As soon as they left Mr McLoughlin's house, with much shaking of hands and apologies for putting him to so much trouble, and telling him how welcome he was to drop in any time he happened to be in the city, her parents drove back to Derry in tight-lipped silence. Ellie could see her mother's knuckles white against the black steering-wheel. She shrank low in the back seat of the car, dreading the show-down that was bound to come.

As the lights of the city appeared, her father seemed to breathe more easily. He turned round and said between clenched teeth,

"What in God's name possessed you to go off gallivanting like that without telling anyone where you were – you could have been killed. And going into a stranger's house – have you never listened to a word we've been telling you? There are men, women and children being murdered in this country every day. You don't know who that man was."

Ellie felt her lip tremble. "I just went for a ride on my bike. I wanted to see the shipwreck. I thought I'd be home before you."

"And that's another thing – your good bike . . . The house insurance probably won't cover that, you know, not when you lost it across the border . . . Jesus Christ, Ellie, we can't afford to buy you a new bike every time you decide to hurl it into the sea . . . "

"I didn't hurl it into the sea," Ellie began lamely but it was no use. Her father turned away from her.

They bumped over the ramps in front of the police station, in dark shadow behind its high protective walls and coils of barbed wire. Caught in the car's dipped headlights was a foot patrol of soldiers. As they drove towards them, the man in the rear slowly turned to face them, his rifle pointing directly at Ellie's mother. Although she had seen this a hundred times and knew it was nothing to worry about, Ellie shuddered. Neither her father nor mother paid any attention to the pointing gun. Ellie turned around in her seat and looked at the soldiers through the rear window as the car swept past.

"Must be time for the news," said her mother, snapping on the car radio. There had been another car bomb in Belfast. Two men had been killed. The usual people made the usual condemnations . . .

Alone again in her bedroom, Ellie could not sleep. She kept replaying in her head the ripping sound of the earth as it gave way behind her and the thud as it crashed into the sea. She could not shake off the ghostly apparition at the cliff-top or the creepy words that Mr McLoughlin had used, the sod of death. The very sound of it made her flesh crawl. She got out of bed and walked over to the window-sill where she had placed the silver coin and the little ivory-coloured object she had found among the fallen boulders.

Carefully she placed both her finds under the pillow. Tomorrow, when the parents had calmed down a bit, she would show them the coin. Maybe they could help her find out how old it was and if it was Viking as she suspected it must be. God, she said, let me not dream tonight. I'm so tired, I feel I could sleep forever. She pulled the duvet right up over her head and closed her eyes, but sleep would not come.

The picture of Harald unfolding and standing before her at the edge of the cliff haunted her. "Who are you?" she said. "What do you want?" Angrily she pushed off the bedclothes and went again to the window to look down the river. I shall have to speak to someone, she thought, someone who knows about the Vikings. Raping and pillaging, that's all she ever remembered hearing about them. Whatever pillaging was. It was funny that her name, McLoughlin, meant Son of the Viking, and that that nice old man had the same name. He had said Viking ships had come into all the loughs and rivers along the north coast. Maybe these visions she was having, the fire on the beach, the ships on the river and this Harald, whoever he was, were just garbled stories she had once been told back in primary school? It was possible they had floated back up to the surface of her mind and invaded her dreams. Dreams were peculiar. She had always dreamt about the daftest things anyway.

No, the voice within her replied, *this is real.*

Ellie shifted uneasily in her bed and glanced nervously towards the window where she had seen the blond-haired figure the night before. No-one. Her hand slipped under the pillow and clenched her treasures from the beach.

Ellie, Ellie, Ellie, the voice in her head began. *I have no peace . . .*

"All right, Harald Olafsson," she said sharply, sitting up and addressing the empty window ledge, "if you are really there and trying to talk to me, stop being so devious. Make me understand what you want."

Chapter 6

"When the wind is from the north
The fierce and shadowy waves go forth
Leaping, snarling at the sky,
To the southern world they fly
and the confines of the earth."
Storm at Sea, Anon, Trans. Frank O'Connor

She was at the doorway of a low timber house. The stench coming from inside almost made her gag but she forced herself to walk in, peering through the smoke from the fire that smouldered dully in a low hearth in the centre of the room. There was no furniture but for a few crudely carved benches around the walls. As her eyes adjusted to the darkness she saw that there were two men in one corner, playing some sort of game with dice and counters, taking it in turn to throw the dice onto a gaming-board. Neither looked up as she approached, as if she were not there at all, as if she were a ghost passing through rooms, invisible to their occupants.

She entered the inner room. An old woman was squatting on the beaten earth floor, surrounded by a low heap of antlers, her back to Ellie. There was a regular scraping sound as if she were whittling at something in her hand. As Ellie bent over her to see, the old woman turned and gazed at her with wild staring eyes. In her hands she held the thing Ellie had found on the beach, except that it was no longer broken. It was a pretty cream coloured comb with fine teeth and a graceful arched back with spirals carved at either end.

"This is my gift for Harald," said the old hag, "for it was he who brought down the deer last summer. He will carry this with him from the land of his birth."

In the other room, the two men broke out in sudden raucous laughter, slapping their large hands against their thighs.

Ellie ran stumbling from the over-heated suffocating hovel, the smells of stinking fish and damp earth filling her nostrils, but was immediately chilled to the bone. She found herself standing on an outcrop of rock, overlooking a narrow steep-sided fjord. She knew it must be morning but the sun had not risen. Far-off, out to sea, eerie green swirls of light swept across the empty dome of the sky. The lights flickered and vanished, then reappeared floating like lazy streamers in a slow kaleidoscope swirl. She stood, mesmerised, even though in her night-clothes she was frozen to the bone.

The Northern Lights, said a now familiar voice beside her. Ellie turned slowly to see Harald beckoning her to follow him. *Come away with me.*

She shifted restlessly in her bed, drawing the covers closely around her for she felt suddenly very cold. In that half state of consciousness between sleep and wakefulness, she half-considered getting up and putting on her dressing-gown in case she was to be drawn back into the cold far north. She was sleepily aware of the cat jumping off the bed and sharpening his nails on the carpet, before she gave herself up again to her dreams.

She followed Harald as he ran ahead of her. A tiny landlocked harbour lay beneath the steep sides of the fjord where a fleet of six monster-headed sailing ships were lying at anchor. They were berthed side-on, so the men who were loading on the supplies had to pass them from hand to hand across the ships until all were laden. Ellie watched them heaving lumpy parcels to those on board, heaps of furs and the skins of seals and reindeer, tusks of ivory and whale bone. Next came huge coils of ropes, then barrels of food and water. Harald jumped on to the boat nearest the shore and leapt across each one in turn until he stood at the rudder of the furthermost ship.

And then they were gliding off between the steep-sided cliffs alive with the clamour of thousands of nesting sea-birds. Once again, Ellie had the sensation that she was floating, hovering above the fleet as the sailors followed their course out on to the open sea and turned due west, sailing with a fair wind that never dropped until they passed the Shetland Islands and then, as she now knew they would, turned southwest for Ireland and the estuary of Lough Foyle.

Images raced through her mind, each dream sequence like the chapter of a book, sometimes moving the story along, sometimes back-tracking to fill in a little more detail. She saw Harald and his companions drawing down the square sails over the decks of the ship as night fell to lie exhausted beneath their makeshift tent until dawn. She heard the sad haunting music of the whales who followed the ships and the singing of the men as they worked, deep-throated songs which echoed across the ocean like the growls of far-off barking dogs.

Ellie, a voice called out, *look for me.*

The pictures in her head faded and there was silence. Ellie found herself once more lying alone in her room with the light of a pale silvery moon falling across her bed. Suddenly the cat jumped to the floor, hissing and growling. Ellie sat up sharply.

"What is it, pussy?" she asked.

The cat ignored her, but moved sideways towards the window, still hissing and spitting as before, his tail and back arched aggressively, his lips drawn back to expose his sharp teeth.

As Ellie threw off the bed clothes and got out of bed to reassure the cat, the figure of the Viking Harald slowly took shape in front of her. He stood at the window, his back towards her as if he were looking out onto the curving river beneath, then slowly turned to face her. The cat gave a loud mew of alarm and fled from the room. As Ellie turned to watch it go, she saw her reflection in the mirror of the dressing-table, and behind her, the dormer window. It took only a split second to see that there was no reflection of the figure at the window. More slowly this time, Ellie turned back towards the window. The figure, bathed in moonlight, still stood there quite motionless before her.

For a brief second or two, Ellie thought of her parents sleeping in the bedroom below. She could call out to them – but it was already too late. She lifted her eyes and met Harald's. His eyes were like jewels, of a blue so intense she could not bear to look away from them.

"Who are you?" she croaked. "What do you want from me?"

His voice when he spoke was young and strong.

Ellie, I knew you would answer me. Only you will know where to find me now. There is very little time left. I shall have no peace until you find me.

"But who are you?" asked Ellie again. "What do you mean that I must find you?"

You know who I am. I have told you I am Harald Olaffson of Bergen in Norway.

The figure lifted his arm as if he was going to touch her but Ellie stepped back.

Do not be afraid. I will not harm you.

"But why have you come here? Why are you haunting me?" she managed to whisper.

Listen to what I have to say, replied Harald *and then you will know what you have to do.*

Chapter 7

So when this man died they said to his slave women:
"Which of you wants to die with him?" One of them
answered, "I do." From that moment she was put in the
constant care of the two other woman servants who
took care of her to the extent of washing her feet with
their own hands. They began to get things ready for the
dead man, to cut his costume and so on, while every
day the doomed woman drank and sang as though in
anticipation of a joyous event.

Contemporary eyewitness account of a Viking cremation
by Arab ambassador Ibn Fadlan in 922

"In the country where I grew up, locked into its seasons
of eternal night or eternal day, there was little land
between the ice-capped peaks and the sea," Harald
began. "Famine stalked our people. For many
generations, men had left to seek new land and settle in
the Viking cities of England and Ireland. And so, my
father, Olaf of the Nine Sea-Battles, also built a ship,
seventy feet long from stem to stern, with a keel hewn
from a single oak trunk. It carried sixteen oars on each
side and a prow in the form of a rampant dragon to
ward off evil. He led a fleet of six ships to Ireland

hoping to find land to graze our animals, timber to build new homes and enough fish in the sea and birds in the air to hunt and fill our bellies. Of those who travelled with us, some were kin-folk including my cousin Ragnall who led the *Gokstad*; others were men who had already travelled far and wide and who had fought beside my father at sea; and there were others, new to travel but eager for new beginnings away from the cold, the overcrowding and the hunger that had until then been their lot.

My father named his ship the *Sleipnir*, which is the name of the eight-legged horse of Odin, the god of power and wisdom and also of battle.

You have seen how we came here for I have shown you in your dreams how we crossed the Northern Ocean and into the lough. Our journey was swift and uneventful until we came to the narrow entrance to the lough. The *Sleipnir* was out in front, leading the way, when I saw floating on the water a dark mass of what I thought was wreckage. We slowed down to see what it was for a wrecked boat might provide us with useful spoils – but as I leant out to prod it with my boathook, it came alive, flailing out at me with many long arms and squirting thick black ink in all directions, so that we were half blinded by its poison. Its arms became entangled in the oars of the *Sleipnir*, dragging us down so far into the water that the sea threatened to engulf us all. My father ordered his men to seize their axes and swords, which they bravely did, lashing out at the creature's tentacles until at last it sank wounded beneath the surface of the waves."

"What was it?" asked Ellie.

"It was a draken," Harald replied, "a monstrous sea

creature I had often heard of from homecoming sailors, though none of us on the *Sleipnir* had ever seen such a thing. We continued our journey through the mouth of the lough, somewhat unsettled at having come across such a bad omen at our journey's end, with each man scanning the sea for further portents of bad fortune. Where the lough narrowed, we followed the river as far as the settlement on the island that is known as Daire Calgach." Harald turned his back to Ellie and pointed across the river to the sleeping city of Derry on the bank opposite.

"There was a small church there, a monastery, with many round thatched dwelling-houses on the high dry land all about it but the monastery was not a rich one and we had come neither to raid it nor to take slaves as earlier expeditions from Norway had done. What we wanted was to trade and make a new home for ourselves and our families. We had with us thick skins of reindeer and bear, strong ropes of whale-hide and walrus, ivory tusks beyond price, besides combs and ornaments of antler and feather.

In the darkness that comes before dawn, our ships sailed silently forward, unseen by anyone within the sleeping city. My father, Olaf, bade the men to bear towards the eastern side of the river. There were no dwellings that we could see there, only dense woods covering the hillsides, and my father intended to draw up our longboats on the shingle and wait until morning before we sent a messenger into the city. When dawn broke the people within would be overawed at the sight of our boats proudly drawn up on the opposite shore, but would know we had no violent intention or we might have murdered them in their beds and made free with the silver and gold of their churches. In any case, Daire Calgach was but a small settlement, and we were so many, thirty-two in each of our six ships.

The air had been growing heavy and close all that night and even as we made to land, the first raindrops fell. My father had earlier chosen me to be the first to leap on to the land where we would settle. I had just stepped on to the side of the *Sleipnir* to drop down when there was a shout from behind me.

'Fenri,' roared a voice, 'beware of Fenri.'

Out of the oak woods above us came a dark long-haired wolf who stood and looked down on us. It threw back its head and howled long and loud. At the sight of this, (for surely it was a bad omen for our people that Fenri, the wolf who had swallowed up the god Odin in his great battle against the powers of evil, had appeared at the precise moment of our disembarking) Olaf ordered me to stay. But the oarsmen, alarmed at the mention of Fenri, had already roughly seized their oars to pull away. As the boat lurched, I lost my footing and fell clumsily into the waters of the river." Harald turned once more and pointed to the river bank below. "There you can see the spot where I fell."

Ellie shivered but did not move closer to the window to look down.

Ghosts usually haunt the scene of their death, she thought, he must have drowned there, but the figure continued to speak as if he had read her mind.

"No, I did not drown but thereafter neither peace nor a long life were to be mine. There was a resounding clap of thunder and the sky darkened as if something had passed in front of the moon, blotting out all light. The river closed over me, its treacherous current dragging me out into the middle of the stream. Weeds knotted around my legs so I could scarcely swim. I prayed, give me strength, O Thor, and deliver me from your anger, and struck out back towards the river bank. A long shaft of silver lightning lit up the river at that moment and I could see that my father's ship had already turned, for such is the art of our boat-builders that our ships can be turned in an instant, even into the wind, and be off before our enemies have sounded their alarms. I could see its mighty oars smiting the water so fiercely that it seethed white with foam."

"They left you here?" asked Ellie.

Harald shook his head.

"I dived beneath the surface of the water and swam back to the eastern shore, opposite the island monastery. Someone there had raised the alarm and I could hear bells ringing out, loud and furious. I pulled myself on to the bank and looked back. Three of the ships were making for the opposite bank where tiny figures had already appeared at the earthen enclosure of the monastery, raining arrows upon the longboats. The other three ships were in mid-river, the men at their oars, apparently heading back to sea.

I thrust my way into the woods, pushing aside the low-hanging branches of the oak trees which came back and whacked me in the small of my back. Clumps of stinging nettles burned my bare legs but there was no time to stop lest anyone had seen me land. With every step I took deeper into the oak grove, I could think of nothing but the face of my father as the *Sleipnir* drew away from me. He was screaming something but his words were carried off in the wind. I kept running, not knowing where my steps were leading me, nor caring, conscious only that I had been abandoned in a hostile country, until I became aware of other people moving among the trees around me. I slowed my pace and dropped to a crouch behind a large oak from where I could look down through a clearing to the river-bank below. There was the most frantic chorus of shouts and wailing. Other running figures began to appear, their dark shadows darting in and out of the shelter of the mighty oak trees. A group of women holding small children in their arms ran past me, only an arm's length from where I lay hidden. The very air seemed to stink of fear.

"The Vikings have landed, they have beached their ships," came a shout.

"From the fury of the Norsemen, O Lord, deliver us, for they will surely overrun all before them."

"How are we to withstand them?" came another voice. "Wave after raging wave, they come to steal our gold and take us into slavery."

Behind me, I heard a stifled scream and turned around. A young girl had stumbled over a tree root and lay spread-eagled on the ground. For a moment, no more, her eyes met mine. Her mouth opened in a silent scream and her eyes grew wide with horror. I placed my fingers across my lips, praying that she would make no sound, for, had she but known it, I was as alarmed for my safety as she was for hers. I began to move away from her, holding her gaze in mine and spreading my hands open to show I had no arms and had no wish to harm her.

At that moment there was a violent shaking among the branches between me and the river. The trees parted and the berserks came into view.

The berserks were the most violent warriors who had travelled with the fleet my father had brought to Ireland. They were the strongest men among us, terrible to see, and so fearless, half-mad I would say, that they would go into battle wearing no armour and naked to the waist. They were wild-eyed men who struck fear into all who saw them, even their own kinsmen. Several of them had already travelled out of Bergen with my father on earlier fleets and I had grown up with tales of their exploits in battle. They were men to have on your side – or, if you were unlucky enough to have them as your enemy, to fear as bloodthirsty slayers. I should have known my father would send them back to rescue me. As soon as he saw me, Sitric Finehair waved his axe above his head and bellowed at me to go back towards the river.

One of the others rushed forward and seized the girl who had fallen on the forest floor. He pulled her roughly to her feet and dragged her back towards the river-bank. I could hear her screams echoing through the woods as she was carried off. I turned in haste to follow them.

I had hardly gone more than a few yards when an arrow whistled by my ear and fell at Sitric's feet. He stooped to pick it up and snapped it in two. Behind us there was a slight movement in the trees. It was still dark and raining heavily but there had been no more thunder since the clap that had resounded as I fell into the river. Sitric's eyes darted around the forest, straining to detect every change of light, every moving shadow that might reveal where our attackers hid. Then out of the silence there came a low rumble that grew and grew and swelled into a terrifying roar, as if the god Thor himself was hammering the daylight out of the sky. Long streaks of crackling lightning lit up the woods and the river. In that sudden flash of light, I saw the *Sleipnir* approaching the bank, its long dog-neck raised proudly towards the heavens. My father was coming.

At the same moment Sitric Finehair let out a wild blood-curdling roar and raced out of cover past the massive oaks, his long-handled axe circling above his head. His screams brought others out of their hiding places and all scattered among the trees, whooping and jeering.

The first screams of the dying reached my ears very soon. Unarmed as I was, I made my way back alone towards the river, intending to reboard my father's ship and take whatever weapons I could find there. At the river bank, I stooped behind a rock and looked around. Three of our ships, the *Sleipnir*, the *Asgard* and the *Dreki*, lay at anchor by the water's edge, empty but for a handful of men guarding the stores and the few women who had travelled with us.

On the far side of the river, the other three ships of our fleet had drawn up on the opposite shore. Dawn was breaking so even at that distance and in the teeming rain, I could make out our men with their round white shields and long broad swords bearing down on the Irishmen on the ramparts of the city. But the curse of Fenri lay upon us for, greater in number though we were, many would be dead before the day had ended." Harald sighed and turned away from Ellie to look across the river.

"Go on," said Ellie softly.

Harald's blue eyes turned and held hers once more.

"We Norsemen are brave warriors, not softened by

easy living. Poverty, famine, the icy breath of the north winds which blew across our land and killed our crops, these are what drove my people to seek new homes in Ireland. But we had pride too, a spirit that yearned for adventure and sent us out to seek new horizons. We were never afraid to fight to hold on to what we seized. We had a scorn for death and for all men who lacked stomach for the fight."

Yes, thought Ellie, cruel, bloodthirsty men.

"No," said Harald, once more answering her thoughts, "bold and resolute, fighting for our own people that they should live. But I curse the day I set foot in this place for I was damned before the day was out, and was soon to be outcast by the very men who had taken me to this country."

"You were given as a hostage?" asked Ellie.

Again, Harald shook his head, as if impatient at her interruptions.

"I ran to the *Sleipnir* and called to the guard who stood at the side-rudder to hand me down sword, axe and knife. Until that day, I had never taken up arms against a living person but I knew I would not shrink from my duty if I had to. My father, Olaf of the Nine Sea-Battles, the guard told me, had gone into the woods in search of me.

As I moved back into the dark shadows of the oak woods, following the cries of battle, I saw there had already been much blood shed. A trail of blood led me to a clearing where several bodies lay as they had fallen, some lifeless, others left for dead but still groaning in their final agonies. Some way off, lay a body on its back, its skull almost parted. His long limbs were at once familiar to me. I knelt down, and rolled the body over. It was my father, Olaf of the Nine Sea-Battles, hacked to death by strangers on a foreign soil." Harald's voice trembled and he stopped speaking. Ellie, her stomach heaving at the violence, the butchery of Olaf's death, said nothing either but stared at her hands and waited for Harald to take up his story again.

"I screamed as I had never done before or since, the cry rising from my belly in fury and pain, the war-cry of all my people down the generations. Who had committed this evil deed, I knew not, but I swore over my father's still warm body that I would avenge his death. I raised my sword above my head and plunged into the battle.

I killed a man that day. Who he was, whether slave or of royal blood, I have no way of knowing. I cared not if he had children who loved him, or a woman to weep over him, I only knew that my father was dead and that nothing but more blood spilled would satisfy me. We fought hard and long on the east side of the river and took no hostages, none but the young girl the berserk had taken earlier to the river-bank. When all our enemies lay either dead around us or had scattered deep into the woods, my cousin Ragnall and I carried my father's broken body back to the *Sleipnir*.

Just as we laid him out upon a bench at the rear of the ship, a great cry went up that echoed across the black expanse of river between us and Daire Calgach. Two of the ships that had drawn in on the far shore were pulling away, their oars smiting the river so that it boiled white with surf. A grey column of smoke was rising from the third, the *Dragon of Bergen*, yellow flames licking around its prow. (It was Fergal, son of Domnall of the royal kings of Aileach, who, in the heat of the battle, had climbed aboard the *Dragon*, emptied it of all its goods and set it alight.) More than thirty Bergen men were slain in the battle on the western side of the river, their bodies broken and tossed into the river and the contents of their ship confiscated and divided among the Irish lords.

In haste then, the men of the *Sleipnir*, the *Dreki* and the *Asgard*, leapt to the rowing benches and seized oars. Under a volley of burning arrows we turned our ships and, tired out as we were, turned back down the river until at last we could set sail again. There was scarcely a sound on board as we passed through the narrow place where the salt and fresh waters meet and we came to that wide white strand at the very edge of the Northern Ocean.

There Sitric bade us stop for he had seen a mighty omen. On the cliff above us, stood a huge black raven. Now the god Odin, the mighty and all-seeing god of wisdom and battle has many ravens who fly into the world every day to gather knowledge of mortal man. Each night, the ravens return with their news to the great hall of Valhalla, where warriors slain in battle dwell after death. Where Sitric sighted the raven, he said, there we must bury the body of my father and offer sacrifices for those of our men whose broken bodies lay lost at Daire Calgach. The god Odin had decreed it to be so.

And so, we drew in to the white strand, according to our custom.

We threw overboard the pillars of my father's seat, that is the beams that surrounded his seat as master of our house and of the fleet, and let them drift ashore at the will of the gods. We waited while the waves lifted them on their shoulders and carried them in to land. Then the five ships that remained drew up on the wide beach, there being no natural harbour at this place, where we dragged them into a circle within which we could defend ourselves from attack during the night.

My father, Olaf of the Nine Sea-Battles, was carried ashore. We laid him first in a shallow grave which we covered with sods of turf and soil torn from the summit of the cliff where Sitric had first seen the raven. There he was to lie while his grave goods were prepared and the funeral ship made ready for the cremation in ten days' time.

When our task was done, I walked to the place where my father's slave women and servants were waiting and said, 'Which of you wishes to die with him?' For when a chieftain like my father dies, it is the custom that his wife or one of his slaves should go with him to paradise.

'I shall,' said Gudrun, stepping forward and falling at my feet. 'I shall die with him.'

Then two of the servants took her away to the water's edge and washed her and gave her nabid which is a sort of drink that we have, that intoxicates and makes men forget their pains, and they stayed with her until the day of the cremation came. I could hear her singing as she was led away as if she longed for the day of her death to come . . .

As night drew in around us, I lay on my back looking at the stars, the sky so similar to that which hangs over my home at Bergen, thinking how different our first night on land might have been if my father had not been so cruelly taken from me. He had led us in search of land and trade, not warfare nor destruction, but his death would bring nothing but division and conflict. I knew I was in great danger from many of the older men who would not hesitate to seize my father's power. They would not move against me until my father's funeral was over but move they would. I was young, too young to take my father's place as leader of the fleet and of the settlers, and too isolated there in Ireland with scarcely any people of my own bloodlines. I stood above the beach, looking down on the dark circle of ships and the groups of men sitting around the fires. Should I lay my claim to the *Sleipnir* and return to the famine and hardships of my homeland? Should I follow the older men to Dublin or Strangford, where they would surely go, or sail to Alba where many of our kinsmen already lived by the river Tyne? Or was it best that I stay at Cen-rig and build a new home there as my father had dreamed?

At length I walked back to rejoin my crew in the shelter of the *Sleipnir* but even as I lay there pretending to sleep, I heard the warriors and the berserks arguing and muttering among themselves. 'Harald is but a boy,' someone said, 'unfit to take his father's place, here in a land he does not know.'

'He would be weak, with no stomach for battle.'

'Did he not disobey his father and jump in the river when he told him to stay? "Beware of Fenri," I myself shouted it to him when I saw the wolf, but he did not heed me.'

'He has brought bad fortune down upon us, from the very first when he stirred up the sleeping draken. The deaths of our kin hang upon his head.'

'Let us seize the *Sleipnir* and leave him here.' That was Sitric Finehair, the berserk, his voice hard and brutish like the bark of the wolf, Fenri.

Their voices grew uglier and drunker as they drank nabid until late into the night. From time to time bodies lurched past mine as men left to lie with Gudrun, the slave-woman.

Each day that followed brought more fighting and disturbances. Many of the men swore they would not settle in this place after my father's burial but said we should sail further along the northern and eastern coasts, seeking settlements already under the control of Norsemen. There they declared they would be safe in number and more easily able to trade and make new homes. Others, already sick of their adventure, wished to return to Bergen, and argued that we should do so immediately before the winter storms came. They would stay to prepare the grave-ship and the grave goods, but not a day longer after the funeral rites were done.

On the tenth day, the day of the cremation, we assembled on the edge of the cliff. It was a bitter morning with a cold wind blowing straight in off the sea, stirring the waves up into prancing white horses and throwing thunderous bursts of spray against the cliff for it was the time of the high tide. The grave-ship from the *Sleipnir* had been hauled up from the shore and raised aloft on four stakes of wood under which we had built up a huge store of firewood. A bench covered with the skin of a white bear and cushions of reindeer skin lay in the centre of the grave-ship under a canopy.

Six men had uncovered my father's body from its shallow grave and carried it across the dunes towards the pyre. His body had turned almost black but, because of the cold weather, had not corrupted. He had been dressed in hose and wide trousers, gathered at the knee, and around his shoulders they had placed a long cape made of sable fur, lined with rich silk and fastened at the neck with a large silver brooch. They laid him on the bench on his grave-ship.

Then began a long procession as, one by one, the men of the *Sleipnir* moved forward, carrying nabid and salted meat and onions and rye bread and bowls of hazelnuts and berries. These they placed at his feet so that he should not be hungry on his journey to the great hall of Valhalla to rejoin all the warriors slain in battle and to be with the great Odin, god of wisdom and poetry and war. When they had laid out all the food, and a purse of silver coins, I came forward, bearing in front of me my father's weapons, his long-handled axe and his dagger, his wooden shield and his leather helmet and I placed these by his right hand – all but his sword for I knew he would have wanted me to keep that.

This sword was so richly gilded and inlaid with precious stones it was considered to be the best sword in Bergen. I had taken it from beside my father's dead body the day that he was killed and had put it on as a symbol that I had assumed my father's authority on the same day that we had landed at Cen-rig. My father had carried it at all of the nine great sea-battles that gave him his name and it had brought nothing but good fortune to him. His father, my grandfather Harald Olafsson whose name I carry, had made that sword himself, for he had learnt the art of sword-making when he lived among the Franks.

When I had placed the weapons by his side, Ivar, the master of the *Asgard*, then approached, a cock and hen in either hand, and he slit their throats and let the blood

61

flow onto the earth and then threw them on to the floor of the ship. And I was sad and ashamed that my father was dishonoured for we had no more animals to sacrifice. For a man of his rank, we should have slain dogs and horses and cows and pigs and made sacrifice in honour of the gods but, alas, we had none of these.

Then Gudrun, the slave-woman who wished to die with my father, was led towards the ship by the oldest slave-woman, a woman of grim appearance, who had been preparing Gudrun for her death for ten days past. Gudrun, pale and staggering a little, removed the bracelets from her wrists and gave them to the old woman. She stooped and took off the silver anklets she wore and passed them among the other slave-women who embraced her, wailing and weeping all the time. One handed her a beaker of nabid which she drank in one draught and threw the beaker to the ground. My eye caught hers and she looked completely bewildered as if she scarcely knew where she was or what was about to become of her. Then a number of men moved forward carrying wooden shields and sticks. At a signal from one of them, the old slave-woman bound Gudrun's hands and feet with cords. Then four men, two at her feet and two at her head, lifted her on to the grave-ship where they laid her out of sight under the tent. The old slave-woman climbed up. I saw the glint of a dagger before I turned away.

All the men present began to beat their shields, louder and louder, in a frantic rhythm, to deaden the shouts of Gudrun. They did not want the other slaves to hear them and be afraid, lest they should not be willing to die with their masters when their turn came."

Yes, thought Ellie as she listened to Harald, this was

my dream about the beach, the men pounding their shields, the frantic wailing women and the smell of burning ash on the wind.

"As the old slave-woman lowered herself from the ship, I, being the closest kinsman, took a piece of wood and lit it and thrust it into the pile of wood on which the grave-ship rested. Then others followed me, coming forward with branches and burning brands and throwing them on to the pyre. The fire quickly took hold with the strong wind from the sea fanning the flames, so that first the wood and then the ship and the tent and lastly, my father, Olaf of the Nine Sea-Battles, and Gudrun, his slave-woman, were engulfed and rapidly carried to paradise.

And so ended my tenth day in Ireland."

Harald paused.

Ellie lifted her face to look at his, but did not dare move or speak lest she startle him and make him disappear. She even wondered if he had forgotten her. He had fallen into a trance as he stared down the river towards the sea. *Only you will know where to find me.* The words repeated themselves in her head. Is this it? she thought. Have I found him? Or is there something else I must do? Some thing he wants me to do?

As if he had understood her thoughts, Harald slowly turned his head, meeting her gaze with his penetrating blue eyes. He began to speak again.

Chapter 8

> The sea cast up a woman whose hair was one hundred
> and ninety feet . . . the length of her plaits were
> seventeen feet . . . the length of her nose seven feet . . .
> and altogether she was as white as a swan.
>
> The *Annals of Ulster*

"The next morning, Sitric Finehair, the leader of the berserks, came to me and told me they were leaving, taking the *Dreki* with them, and any man from the other ships who wished to follow them. Then Ivar of the *Asgard* said he too was leaving, that the land was poor and unprotected, and it would be better for all of us to sail around the coast and make for Dublin. A clamour then arose, with even the men of my own ship, the *Sleipnir*, demanding we all should leave, saying that without the men of the *Dreki* and the *Asgard*, we were too few to stay. Others muttered among themselves, too ashamed to speak their minds to me, saying that my father had chosen ill in coming to Lough Foyle to settle.

But I would not agree to leave. What is a man without his family? Even if a man perishes, his family must not abandon him nor make him feel so forsaken that he must walk after death to tend his own grave. No,

I argued, we must stay and build our homes here on the coast where my father had led us and where his ashes lay, but I was too young and too recently catapulted into command by my father's untimely death for them to listen.

By midday when the sun had climbed directly overhead, they had decided. Three ships were to sail at once – the *Dreki*, the *Asgard* and the *Walrus* – taking any man who wished to leave without fear of retribution. They left us what stores and provisions they could afford and several of the slave-women besides, intending to land whenever and wherever it pleased them as they made their way to Dublin, seizing food and supplies as they needed them. About fifty men stayed behind with me, some of them free men who had sailed from Bergen on the *Sleipnir*, as well as Ragnall, my cousin, the master of the *Gokstad* and several of his crew. We kept back a number of the slave-women, including the girl the berserk had seized from the oakwoods of Daire Calgach. She had not spoken since her capture but had recoiled from every man and woman who had come near her. The only time I had heard her make a sound was on the day of the funeral. She had been with the slave-women at the summit of the cliff, watching what was happening with wide frightened eyes as if she had never seen the like of us before. As I thrust the first burning branch into the funeral pyre, she had begun to moan in a low pitiful voice, repeating the same thing over and over to herself in a language we could not understand, and crossing her forehead and body with her right hand.

That first night that our small group was left alone, the sky seemed to glow with comets. Bright stars fell from the heavens, trailing tails of fire behind them. We stood by the water's edge, watching them in silence. A dangerous mood hung over us, fuelled by these strange heavenly phenomena, and by our sense of isolation. The women shrieked and wept, crying out 'what is to become of us' until one of the men, exasperated, struck out at them.

I walked away and stood beside my father's grave at the very edge of the land, gazing out upon the ocean and the sky. The ashes of the ship had been covered over with soil and flat stones but the mound still gave off heat as if below the surface the ashes still glowed. As I watched the shooting stars falling into the sea, I began to notice a long dark shape just below the surface of the water, a short distance from the shore. At first I thought it must be a rock that we had not seen because of the recent high tide – until I realised that the shape moved. The waves picked it up, tossing it forward, then dragging it back out to sea again. I ran down to the strand and called to some of my men to follow me, fearing that one of the ships that had departed at midday had perished and was being washed ashore. They peered out into the black and silver ocean as it swelled and tossed before us but saw nothing. One by one, they walked off, until I was left alone and overcome by a deep sense of foreboding.

The following morning, after dawn, I was woken by loud shrieking. I seized my father's sword which lay by my side and stood up, fearing we were under attack.

A small crowd had already gathered at the far end of the beach, and I joined the rest of the men running towards them. People were shouting and yelling and pointing towards the sea so that I supposed something had been washed ashore. The crowd parted for me as I drew near and a terrible hush came down on them. Nothing in my wildest dreams would have prepared me for what I saw next. Half in and half out of the water, lay the figure of a giant woman, cast ashore by the sea. She was as long from head to toe as any of our ships, and her body was altogether whiter than a swan. The tresses of her hair, thick as rope and hanging loose around her face, were as long as three men. She did not breathe but lay as cold as death upon the empty sand with the sea lapping gently around her.

I stood in awe in front of her, wondering from what strange land of giants and monsters she had come, when I became aware that the eyes of all my companions had turned towards me. I turned and scanned their faces. Fear and hatred looked back at me. These people could take no more bad omens – and who could blame them?

My cousin, Ragnall, the master of the *Gokstad*, sailed for Bergen that night, taking thirty men and promising to return before the next full moon with more men and free women to enlarge and protect our settlement. Only twenty men remained with me, among them a handful of former slaves who had fought loyally alongside my father in his sea battles and to whom he had given their freedom. Of the rest, I do not understand why they stayed, perhaps out of laziness, perhaps because they had little to return to Norway for.

Though Ragnall said little to me directly before he left, I knew that I had already lost everything my father had hoped to pass on to me. Ragnall was an ambitious man, and in a war of succession, the loser loses everything. My father was dead. I was young and of no account. I was sure that Ragnall intended to sail to Bergen and seize all my father's property there, his animals and his slaves, everything he had hoped to return for when our settlement was established. Ragnall would be the one who would step into my father's shoes, not I. He would never come back, not before the next full moon, not ever. I am surprised now that he did not put me to the sword before he left.

I stood by the *Sleipnir* and watched them set off under full sail for the low blue island a few hours away on our horizon and beyond that the distant headland of Kintyre. That was the last we were to see of any of them.

Winter came early that year and we were ill prepared for it, with our stores running low and no crop to harvest. There was a great snowfall and such cold that the very birds were falling out of the sky, their wings frozen to their bodies. The rivers, even the sea itself, froze over so that men were able to walk across the mouth of Lough Foyle to the other side. There was an eclipse of the sun and of the moon in the same month. We were sore tried to feed ourselves. When the weather allowed we took the *Sleipnir* and made short raids on the small settlements on Lough Swilly but the people there had as little food as ourselves.

Once we even ventured to the island of Rathlin that lay to the east but as we drew up we could see great devastation on every side. We learned that three Viking ships had attacked weeks earlier, carrying off so many hostages to trade as slaves that there was scarcely an islander left who was not a baby or an old woman in her dotage. These same men had destroyed Dunseverick, on the mainland opposite the island, drowning and beheading all those who lived there, two hundred men in all.

Perhaps it had been Sitric Finehair and the men of the *Dreki*, the *Asgard* and the *Walrus*, I thought. They might have decided to winter over in some safe harbour along the coast before striking for Dublin. We gave up a day or two to look for them, searching every inlet of the northern coast, sailing under cliffs as white as cows' milk, but saw no sign of them. One afternoon, we came to one of the wonders of the natural world, a place sea-farers returning to Bergen had often told us of, where the rocks of the earth are moulded into hundreds and thousands of pillars and columns, and thrones and staircases, as if a jealous god had looked down upon a mortal man's palace and turned it all to stone.

The weather grew steadily worse. For the most part, we stayed at the white strand at Cen-rig, strengthening the shelters we had built beneath the cliff. We lived upon boiled fish and sea-birds and any meat that we could snare, deer sometimes or rabbit, but often we spent the greater part of the day hunting only to bring back less than would feed us all. The men sat in the wooden huts they had built, hungry and out of temper with each other.

"It is no better here than in Norway in the worst winters," they said to me. "Let us load up the *Sleipnir*, set ablaze our houses here and be gone."

"Wait until the spring," I answered, "let us see what the spring brings. No welcome awaits us in Bergen."

Our land, my father had told me before we had left on our journey to Ireland, was like a hive of bees that had grown too big. When that happened, the hive must cast out a new swarm to take wing and seek a new home for itself. I, Harald Olafsson, and my band of twenty, were like that new swarm. We must survive or perish by our own efforts but we could not go back. I understood this better than the older men.

The day of midwinter was approaching, the shortest day of the year. The people were demanding a blood sacrifice, to placate the gods for the crimes we had committed so that they would look with more favour on us in the new year of the sun and bring good fortune to our settlement. At night-time I heard them talking about a sacrifice held every ninth year when ninety-nine animals, equal numbers of horses, dogs and cocks, were sacrificed in honour of the god Frey since Frey is the god who can grant peace and pleasure and fertility.

I gave my permission to set about the preparations but, by then, few paid even lip service to me and many were openly hostile. In the evenings, when we sat down around our fires to eat, they would draw apart from me and set aside only the burnt crusts of bread or the toughest piece of meat for me. I took to sitting up on the cliff, near the mound of earth which now covered my father's grave-ship, with only the Irish slave-girl for company, and both of us unable to understand a word of each other's language.

As the date of the midwinter sacrifice drew near, every man and woman set about the task of trapping. For the first time since they had set foot in Ireland, it seemed as if the settlers' spirits lifted. Each man began making snares and traps to set all about in the dunes. They had decided that ninety-nine animals were to be slain, but since we had no horses nor dogs nor cocks, they were to capture rabbits, hares, birds – both divers and waders – and deer.

On the morning of Midwinter, while it was still dark, I set off to stalk deer with several of the other men in the hills inland. In our country, many chieftains kept herds of reindeer but this was not known in Ireland among the Irish chiefs even though there were deer running wild in all the woods and hills. The Irish valued only cattle and calculated a man's wealth by the number of cattle he owned. Back in Norway, my mother's father had raised four hundred tame reindeer from animals given in tribute to him from the Laplanders who lived in the frozen northern wastelands and these he farmed for their flesh, their milk and their skins. So I had grown up among deer, watching the great males crashing antlers in the rutting season, and later watching milky does trying to lick life into their new-born foals. I also knew how to stalk them, bringing them down as my father had taught me with one well-aimed missile from my catapult.

We walked in silence through the solitary wooded hills. There was no trace of any human habitation in the place, just mile after mile of windswept stony ground. Here and there we came across small white patches of snow untroddden by any living creature. Just before dawn, we came through a clearing in the trees to a shallow stream. I knelt down and examined the muddy bank. There was what I had been looking for – the tracks, both old and fresh, where many deer had forded the stream or stopped to drink running water. We retraced our steps and took cover in the stand of trees behind. As the first cracks of light appeared in the sky, two young female deer came strolling out of the trees and walked towards the water's edge.

We were upon them before they had even caught our scent, throwing our nets of ropes over their heads and tethering them securely together. We were not to kill them for all the creatures for the sacrifice were to be slain together that evening. We began to lead them back down the hills to our settlement at the shore.

We had not got very far when we heard some commotion among the trees and stopped in our tracks. The does were restless, pawing the ground and trying to break free of our ropes. Then we too spotted what they had sensed – a magnificent stag with his back to us. He stood upwind in the shadow of a large rock, so intent on licking salt from the rock that he had not yet picked up the scent of the two does. I covered my lips with my finger to tell the others to be silent and drew my catapult from under my coat. Just as I took aim and let the stone fly up in a wide arc, the two men leading the does moved forward slowly around the outcrop of rock. The stag seemed then to catch their scent. He sniffed the air and gave a couple of low barks. The does moaned in reply, warning him off. And then the stag was running, with the ground pounding beneath his feet and shattering the stillness of the hills. Rabbits skeetered away from their hiding-places and the sky echoed to the screams of a host of birds. I had lost him.

The others moved ahead of me. No one spoke for the rest of our walk back though I seethed with anger, knowing that they had deliberately moved the does to stop me taking the stag.

Back at our settlement, two high posts had been erected on the cliff near my father's burial place and a large stone slab laid on the ground between them. As we approached with the two deer, other men and women were returning with what they had snared and were to offer in sacrifice, foxes and hares, rabbits and diving birds, silver salmon. After their weeks of hardship, there was a new excitement in the air, a feeling that they were on the brink of a new beginning. The animals were counted out solemnly, as they were brought forward to the sacrificial table and offered up to honour Frey, god of fertility, that he might bring peace and well-being to our settlement.

There were ninety-eight in all.

I looked uneasily from face to face, asking for an explanation, asking who had yet to place the ninety-ninth sacrifice. Then the jeering began, the wild roars and ugly laughter as the crowd swarmed around me, pulling me into their centre.

"Will you also die so that we may live?" Their chanting grew louder and louder in my ears, soaring over the sounds of the waves crashing on to the rocks beneath the cliff. I was thrust down on to my knees."

Harald's voice had faded away. Ellie looked over sharply towards the window but there was no-one there, only a pool of pale silver moonlight falling on to the sill. She began to cry softly, letting the tears run down her face as if she wanted to be empty, knowing at last how Harald Olafsson had met his death in Inishowen.

Chapter 9

About one seventh of the land surface of Ireland is
covered by peat, and objects lost or buried in bogs –
especially organic material such as wood, leather, bone
and textiles – are preserved owing to the absence of
oxygen which slows down the process of decay.

Raghnall O Floinn, *Archaeology*, Autumn 1988

There had been no dreams for over two weeks, none at
all. Each night she longed for more of the story to
unfold, for Harald to come back and tell her why he had
come to her but each night sleep came and enveloped
her in a dark black blanket of silence. The early storms
of winter had subsided too and she woke to clear blue
skies as if all the upheaval in the world around her had
vanished with the turmoil inside her head.

One morning a letter arrived from the museum where
she had sent the coin that Mr McLoughlin had given her.

Dear Ellie, she read,

*We are pleased to confirm that the silver coin your friend
discovered on the beach at Ballybeg is indeed from the*

Viking period and was most probably minted in the Viking city of York during the reign of Aulaf. From about the year 900 to the middle of the tenth century the Danish and Norwegian kings of Northumberland produced coins bearing their own names. At that time silver replaced gold as the primary value of metal, much of it brought back by Viking explorers from Arab mines.

It would be hard to speculate as to how the coin came to be where you found it but we do know that Vikings periodically spent the winter along the coast of Northern Ireland and in the rivers and loughs there, although these locations did not develop into towns as in other areas of Ireland.

Please do not hesitate to get in touch with me again if you have any more queries.

The Curator, JD Miller

Ellie could have exploded with excitement. That coin turning up on the beach was no coincidence. It proved that Vikings had been there once – but were they the same Vikings she had dreamed about? Could the silver coin have come from the grave of Olaf of the Nine Sea-Battles? Had Harald really lived there? And how could she prove it? Carefully, she wrapped the white arc-shaped thing she had found among the boulders in tissue paper and posted it off in a padded envelope to JD Miller for identification. It might take a while for a reply, she thought, but in the meantime, she would go back once more to the beach. Perhaps she would be able to find something else, more evidence of Harald's presence. Maybe just being there would help bring back her dreams for she ached with the loss of them.

The following Saturday, she walked across the bridge

and headed for the bus station. She had not told her parents where she was going. There was no sense in worrying them. They were up to high doh with all the recent trouble around Derry. Weeks earlier, a gunman had sprayed a crowd of people in a pub with gunfire and the whole town was edgy. People had stopped going out at night, her father said, for fear of more surprise attacks. In the kitchen, he talked to his friends about peace as if they were preparing for war.

Ellie got off the bus outside the hotel and walked up the hill to Mr McLoughlin's house. The village was very quiet compared to the first time she had been there. Dusty, multi-coloured Christmas lights flashed on and off above the shopfronts of some of the stores but, somehow, they just made the place look even more depressing. Everybody born in this place, Ellie thought, must grow up planning their escape.

At the top of the hill, she walked around the back of Mr McLoughlin's house and peered through the small kitchen window. There were no lights on. The room was empty, and so tidy it almost seemed as if Mr Mc Loughlin had gone away. Someone had cleared away all the clutter that had taken up every surface when she had been there the first time. Even the rusty old rain barrel at the back door where he had filled his kettle to make tea for her the day they had met was full to the brim, its surface covered with a delicate film of thin ice. Disappointed, she turned away, irritated that she wasn't going to be able to tell him the news about the coin, when a battle-scarred old cat appeared at her feet, doing curious figures of eight around her legs, rubbing itself against her. As she bent down to stroke it, she caught the distinct smell of burnt toast coming from the house.

"Burnt your breakfast, Mr McLoughlin, did you?" she said, smiling to herself, pleased with her detective work. She would call back later.

She ran through the untidy backyard, past the heaps of discarded tyres and rusting pieces of cars and lorries and stood up on the low wall overlooking the strand. The old *Viking Warrior* was still there, looking even smaller and bleaker than she remembered it but otherwise the beach was deserted: only a single line of footprints in the sand showed that someone had already gone before her, perhaps the old man himself. She set off across the wide curve of the strand to follow them, treading underfoot the soft squirly casts of sand-worms, skirting the banks of glistening brown seaweed at the high tide line.

Whoever it was who had walked here before her had taken a direct route across the beach to the sand dunes opposite. Ellie began to climb up through the marram grasses and prickly clumps of sea holly, expecting all the time to see the stooped figure of Mr McLoughlin staring out to sea. It was one of those days when the moon floated low in the sky, staying on long after the sun had come out as if it had forgotten to make itself scarce. A biting cold wind was blowing in from the east, clawing at her face as if it wanted to skin her alive.

As she came up onto the highest part of the headland, she saw there was a post with a life-belt tied to it and stopped beside it to catch her breath. The sea beyond was calm and still as glass with a silver light sailing in from the western horizon . . . About a mile away, she could see a small group of mobile homes clinging perilously close to the cliff and wondered if the people who lived in them had moved away. They had been interviewed on television one night, saying they would not leave their homes even if the cliff crumbled away beneath them. Further off on the horizon was the long shape of Rathlin island to the right and in the far far distance, two faint round hills that must be Scotland.

Only you will know where to look. I have no peace until you find me.

Ellie wheeled around at the sound of Harald's voice. She could feel his presence somewhere near her, as real as the smell of the salt and the turf yet she was quite alone. She gripped the life-belt post to anchor herself against the wind and looked around.

Only I will know where to look, she repeated. But *where* was she to look? And what was she to look for anyway? Harald, had he ever existed, had been dead for a thousand years. How could she hope to find any trace of him here?

Remember the coin, said the voice in her head, *you found that.*

Ellie lay down on her tummy and inched herself towards the cliff until she was almost hanging over the very edge. Forty feet below her the sea lapped against the earth and rocks that had fallen down in the storm. She narrowed her eyes, trying to make out any sign of her bike, but it had vanished without trace, long ago dashed to pieces and carried off down the coast by the strong currents. Could there be something else here, she thought. Is that what the voice means? Is there something else here, even more important than the coin?

A few metres away, a trickle of small stones fell away and plummeted to the ground beneath. Ellie drew back from the edge and got to her feet. She stood with her back to the sea, scanning the contours of the land for any sign of the terrible events that she had dreamed of, the cremation and burial of Olaf of the Nine Sea-Battles and the sacrifice of his slave Gudrun, but there was nothing there but a wild windswept expanse of bad land, pitted and scarred with wide trenches. Nothing except a conviction that her dreams were real. This is where he was murdered, she said aloud, and that other voice, the voice that had been haunting her for many weeks, repeated its mournful dirge.

Only you will know where to find me.

"But I don't," she wailed into the wind, thinking how unfair it was that when such a violent thing happens, it doesn't leave some sign – like that lingering smell of burnt toast that hangs around a kitchen long after the toast has been thrown away. If only there was some sort of scar on the land, or ripples of energy radiating out from it, then anyone who came upon the scene would understand that something awful had taken place there. But that didn't happen. On television and in her own city, she had seen the sites of too many murders and violent deaths. Places where the most awful things had happened quickly returned to normal. People forgot. They forgot things they had promised never to forget. For a few weeks you passed the piles of flowers left by stunned well-wishers. After another few weeks, the flowers were gone and passers-by tossed chocolate wrappers and cigarette butts where men had lain dying. *The sod of death.* Mr McLoughlin's strange words came back to her and a shiver ran down her spine. The sod of death, the place where fate intended you to die.

She began to move slowly around, drawing away from the high dry ground by the cliff edge to the peaty places lower down. Bog holes pitted the earth, many of them full of blackish water, some with a frosting of ice which the weak sun had not yet melted. She turned over several flat stones like the ones she had seen on Mr McLoughlin's kitchen floor but found nothing but a small white skull at the entrance to a rabbit burrow.

This *had to be* the place that Harald had described so vividly in her dreams, the cliff where the midwinter sacrifice had been held. His distant disembodied voice echoed in her ears.

Ellie, I have no peace, only you will know where to find me. Save me before I disappear for ever.

Slowly she turned around. Up at the very edge of the cliff stood the wooden cross-bar post with the heavy life-belt tied to it. It tilted and swayed drunkenly in the chill wind as if it too might give way at any moment and fall off into the sea beneath. Ellie shivered, remembering the night she had lost her bicycle, had nearly lost her own life. Was it not there, she thought, right at the edge, where the greenish light had appeared and the figure of Harald had unfolded.

Whatever Harald wants me to find has to be here, she thought, near the edge. There is something here that is in danger of falling away into the sea. That is what he means.

She began to run back, running up the slope, with the images of Harald from a hundred dreams racing across her mind's eye. There was no barrier between them, just an imaginary line at the edge of time, that divided their parallel worlds. He was as real to her at that moment as any of the living who shared her world. She raced back up the slope towards the cross but as she drew near, the same eerie green light began to radiate at the horizon, just as it had the night she had lost her bike. She stopped short and watched. A shadowy figure took shape in front of her, rising up from the ground, unfolding its long limbs, until it hovered at the very point where land and sea collided. Harald's long white face looked down on hers, the membrane of skin stretched taut like the fleshless face of a dying man, but his voice when he spoke to her was strong and alive.

Here they murdered me, Ellie. Now find me.

And he stretched out his arm, beckoning her to come forward. This time she did not shrink from him but moved confidently closer.

She flung herself to the ground and began to pull away the clumps of grass at the base of the post to expose the spongy turf beneath. The post tilted a little where the awful weather recently and the erosion at the cliff edge had loosened it. Narrow cracks and fissures in the earth radiated out from the post to the land's edge, unsettling reminders of the power of the sea and wind here at the very edge of the country. It would not be long before the constant battering and buffeting by the sea brought this part of the headland crashing to the strand beneath. She stood up and with freezing fingers untied the heavy lifebelt, almost buckling beneath the weight of it as it fell into her arms. She heaved it on to the ground a few feet away and leant against the post. It shifted and wobbled a little more, forcing the fibres of turf apart with a ripping sound. Boldly, she seized the wooden shaft of the post with both hands and shook it, backwards and forwards, one, two, three, four, five times, then rocked it to left and right, until, at last, the post gave way and both it and Ellie fell sideways on to the ground. A hole, almost a metre deep, had opened up. Ellie peered into its murky darkness.

Gingerly she put in one arm and patted the ragged sides of the trench with cautious fingertips. At the base of the trench her hand rubbed against something round and hard. She pulled away as if stung by a current of electricity and sat back on her hunkers, feeling sick. The wind caught her hair and tossed it back off her face. On it, she caught the smell of blood and felt the wind-borne specks of smoke and ash smear her cheek. She closed her eyes. Then there were men running, red-bearded men, screaming wildly and jeering as they rushed forward, men out of control. She could smell them, smell the wet wool of their clothes, the stale drink on their breath. Ahead of her, at the very edge of the cliff, stood two upright posts framing the setting sun as it descended slowly into the sea, bruising the sky with dark crimson weals. Between them on the ground, (ground that Ellie knew was no longer there, ground that had long ago crashed into the angry sea below in some long forgotten storm), there lay a massive blood-spattered rock laden with the limp bodies of the midwinter sacrifice. Several men circled the altar, holding aloft long flaming torches, chanting. Then they turned towards her, their faces contorted in hatred and excitement. Half-blinded by the light from their torches and by the rays of the dying sun, she caught sight of a glint of metal. Silver sliced the air. There was an astonished scream, and a body was man-handled forward.

Ellie put her hand back in the cleft of the turf and gingerly felt around it. There was something, some thing that did not feel like a rock, something dry and leathery.

She lay down flat and squinted into the hole. She drew her hand along the turf. There was some sort of material embedded in it, something rough, perhaps cloth. Could this be it? Is this what Harald wanted her to find? Had she found a Viking hoard? *Now find me.* The voice echoed in her ears. At last she understood.

She had found the body of Harald Olaffson.

Jumping to her feet, she backed away from the fallen post and began to run down to the strand, half-stumbling across the wide empty expanse of sand to the other side of the bay in her excitement. Mr Mc Loughlin's back door was open. She ran straight in.

"It's me, Ellie," she shouted. "I've found a body up on the cliff."

"Well, you'd better phone the guards," said Mr Mc Loughlin, matter-of-factly, as he came out of his kitchen, wiping wet hands on his trousers and looking not in the least bit surprised to find Ellie had reappeared in his life.

The local garda, Owen McClafferty, was not used to much happening in the way of crime on his patch. A bit of late-night drinking in the local pubs or the odd break-in at the grocery store was as much as he had been led to expect when he had been transferred from his last posting but he had hardly had a day's peace since the night the trawler had been driven aground from the high seas, what with insurance claims and surveyors, newspapermen, people giving out about pollution, sightseers making a nuisance of themselves, even dodgy scrap dealers on the make. What he didn't need was some young one, talking nineteen to the dozen, about finding a body up on the headland.

He put down the phone, ducked beneath the hatch of the counter and came out to the station porch, pulling on his greatcoat. The wind caught him by surprise when he opened the door and he grimly remembered the forecaster saying there were more storms on the way. He looked up towards the cliff and shook his head. If old Matt McLoughlin hadn't backed her up, he would have dismissed the whole thing as some sort of a hoax. He clipped his radio to his coat collar and set off for the top of the cliff.

Ellie and Mr McLoughlin were already standing together by the old lifebelt post when the policeman arrived.

"What's all this about, anyway?" he grumbled. "Somebody's old football, I suppose." He lowered himself on to his knees and peered into the narrow trench. Ellie stood behind him, watching the back of his neck, the red fleshy softness spilling over his stiff shirt collar. The garda shone his torch around the bottom and sides of the hole, now sprinkled with a few flakes of snow.

"There's something in there, all right," said the garda, tipping his hat back to the back of his head and rubbing his scalp with fat fingers, "but I wouldn't like to say what it was. It might just be an old rock, and then I'd look a proper Charlie calling in for extra resources and getting people up here for no good reason and the bad weather closing in around us. What makes you think it might be a body?"

"Please," pleaded Ellie, "just believe me. I know all about it."

"What do you mean you know all about it?" said the policeman sharply.

"I've dreamt about it," said Ellie, knowing how

ridiculous it must sound. "It's . . . it's been here for a long time."

The garda looked from Ellie to Mr McLoughlin, one eyebrow cocked.

"Do you know there are penalties for wasting police time?" he asked.

"We did find a coin, mind you," said Mr McLoughlin, "a Viking coin. It's worth taking a look. It mightn't be a body she has found but, you never know, there could be treasure down there."

Both men gazed into the hole. The garda let his breath out slowly. "I've a spade in the back of the car," he said. "I'll see if I can shift a bit more of the turf but," he stared at Ellie self-importantly, as if it was more than his job was worth talking to her, "if this does turn out to be an old football, I won't hold myself responsible for my language." He awkwardly raised himself off the ground and lumbered heavily over to his car, which was parked a little way off on open ground near the cliff road. Dark wet grassy patches were spreading around the knees of his trousers from where he had been kneeling on the ground.

Ellie looked after him in despair. She was so close to the solution of the mystery that had haunted her all these weeks, only to find herself in the hands of the laziest, fattest, most useless-looking policeman she had ever seen. She went down on her hunkers and felt around the hole in the ground. At the bottom, a smooth round coffee-coloured bump stuck out from the surrounding peat. Ellie picked up the policeman's torch and trained the light squarely on it. She could clearly make out pores of skin.

"Look at that," she said, handing the torch to Mr

McLoughlin, "that's not a football. That's a head."

Matt McLoughlin's face creased with anxiety. He took the torch from Ellie and leaned forward. He ran his fingers over the round bump at the bottom of the trench and over the hairy peat around it.

"I've dreamt about this," Ellie told him. "There is a body there, I know it."

"Whose body are you talking about?" demanded the policeman, coming up behind them and throwing a spade to the ground while he pulled his coat sleeves up to his elbows. "Have we a murder on our hands? If you know something, spit it out." He rubbed his tongue around his lips and swallowed hard. "Has this got something to do with the troubles in the North? Do you know something you're not saying?"

"Take it easy, man," interrupted Mr McLoughlin. "She's only a child."

"Sure, that doesn't mean a thing these days. She might have heard something, seen something."

"It's nothing like that," Ellie insisted. "It's an old body."

Garda McClafferty narrowed his eyes and looked at her coldly. "An old body? You mean sometime in the last twenty odd years, the IRA dumped some poor soul in a shallow grave here in the bog, and it's taken you to find out about it?"

"No, I mean it's a very old body, hundreds of years old."

"Don't be ridiculous. Bodies can't survive for anything like that length of time."

"Well this one has."

"Not another word out of you, do you hear me?" Crossly, the policeman took hold of the spade and thrust it into the torn earth.

"Take it easy, man. You don't want to damage the evidence," said Mr McLoughlin softly. "If there is evidence."

The garda shot him a cold stare but eased the blade more gently into the turf and began to prise away spadefuls of earth, laying them out neatly in a line behind him. Ellie watched him in silence even though her mouth had gone dry and she could hardly keep herself from screaming and yelling with excitement.

After a couple of minutes, the garda stopped to catch his breath. "There does seem to be something odd there," he said, unhappily. "Some sort of material, cloth."

"Maybe you should call the Inspector?" said Mr Mc Loughlin, trying to catch the policeman's eye and nod at Ellie. He didn't want the child to see something that might upset her, give her nightmares. He had suddenly remembered a news item about a local man who had walked out of his house one day and was never seen again. He had probably just cleared off and gone to live in England but, you never knew, maybe he had been murdered. Maybe that was what the girl had found.

"Call the Inspector?" echoed the garda, pressing his weight down on the spade again to lever away the soil. "On what grounds?"

There was a clink as his spade hit metal. Ellie gasped. They all looked at one another.

"Stand well back there," said the garda at last in his strong country accent. "It could be an old mine from the wartime. They still turn up every so often. Dear God, what are we to do?"

All his life flashed across his mind as he imagined himself being blown to smithereens. Ellie and Mr Mc Loughlin had not budged. The policeman rounded on them as another picture formed in his head, as he saw himself standing to attention while the President herself pinned a medal for bravery to his chest.

"Stand back," he snapped. "Do youse want to be killed?"

Then, turning his back to them, he spoke urgently into the radio that was clipped to his collar. "Request assistance" were the only words that Ellie could make out as the crackly static carried the rest of what he said out to sea.

Harald, thought Ellie, you're going to be all right.

Chapter 10

I know not if it will be worth the observing, that a turf-bog preserves things strangely . . . a corpse will ly entirely in one for several years. I have seen a piece of leather pretty fresh dug out a turf-bog that had never in the memory of man been dug before.

Of the Bogs and Loughs of Ireland, W King,
Archbishop of Dublin, 1685

As it turned out, that day was the onset of a bitterly cold spell. The wind shifted, blowing in from the Siberian wastes and plunging most of Europe into a record-breaking cold snap. Ellie and Mr McLoughlin stood guard on the headland all afternoon, ignored or elbowed aside by the new arrivals. More policemen swarmed over the cliff, followed shortly afterwards by other men with expensive overcoats and the trousers of their suits tucked into wellington boots as if they had just rushed from offices. They stood about in small groups, talking in low urgent voices or staring into the hole. An army van drove up. More men arrived and scurried about, ferrying tools and boxes from the boots of cars.

"What are they going to do?" Ellie asked Mr Mc Loughlin.

"They're going to cut out a section of the ground," he replied. "I heard them saying that there are more storms on the way and this section of the cliff face could collapse at any time. They're going to have to move fast if they want to get it out."

Ellie sighed with regret. She felt suddenly deflated as if something she loved had been snatched away from her. Now Harald was in the hands of experts and there was nothing more she could do.

"Have you found anything? Is there a body there?" she asked one of the younger looking men as he passed by her.

"Are you the girl that called out the police?"

Ellie nodded.

"Well, well done. I shouldn't really be telling you this but we're pretty sure there is something very unusual down there."

Ellie and Mr McLoughlin walked back to his house across the strand. As they passed the rusty hulk of the shipwrecked trawler, Ellie stopped and looked up at the carefully painted lettering of its name, *Viking Warrior*.

"Do you believe in dreams?" she asked.

"Do you?" said the old man.

"I dreamt about this beach, you know, before I had ever been here, and about Viking ships, and then when I did come, I met you and you gave me the Viking coin. But it wasn't just a coincidence. The dreams didn't stop. I dreamt about a man who told me stories – and now I've found him, the real Viking Warrior." They had started their ascent of the rutted path to the back yard of Mr McLoughlin's house. "In my dream, he said to me,

Only you will know where to look. He said he could have no peace until I found him."

Mr McLoughlin spoke gently. "Don't, Ellie, there may be nothing there. The time you're talking about was hundreds of years ago. Nothing could survive from then. The body, if there is a body, will have something to do with the trouble in the North. That's only common sense, unfortunately."

"No," said Ellie, vehemently, "you'll see."

The phone was ringing a couple of days later just as Ellie was letting herself into the house. No-one else was at home.

"Ellie?" said an old familiar voice. "I've just been talking to Garda McClafferty."

Ellie's heart started to beat a little faster. "What did he say?"

"Well, it was a body all right," Matt McLoughlin answered. "Once they were sure there were human remains in the soil, they cut out a big rectangular block of peat, wrapped it up in foam and plastic sheeting, and took it away in a police van to the hospital mortuary."

"To a hospital?" asked Ellie. "What for?"

"Well, they have to examine it, I suppose, and find out how the person died – to see if there's been a crime or an accident, and when it happened, all that sort of thing. There are still men working up on the cliff. God knows what else they expect to find."

"And do they know how old the body is? What did they tell you?"

"Well, apparently," Mr McLoughlin's voice faltered for a moment as if he was choosing his words carefully, "the coroner doesn't think it's modern . . . "

Ellie's heart stopped.

" . . . but he has to be sure beyond all doubt before he'll release it to the archaeologists. They're doing more tests on it. Garda McClafferty says there's been talk about bog bodies. Do you know what that means?"

"No," said Ellie, "do you?"

"Well it seems that bodies can be preserved in peat bogs for years and years and years and never rot away. Turf-cutters in England found one a few years ago that turned out to be about two thousand years old."

Ellie held the receiver close to her ear. She could hear Mr McLoughlin's wheezy breathing and knew that he was listening to hers.

"Ellie, are you there?" he asked.

Ellie nodded at her reflection in the hall mirror, forgetting that Mr McLoughlin couldn't see that.

"Are you still there, Ellie? Listen, a man called Miller came to the house to see me this morning. He's one of the people who've been working up on the cliff. He says you wrote to him about the coin I found? Well, he dropped in and he told me to tell you that the other thing you sent him was a comb. It was made of antler." Mr McLoughlin paused. "Probably Viking, he said."

Ellie remembered the old crone in her dream whittling away at a pile of antlers. *This is a comb for Harald for it was he who brought down the deer.*

"Are you there, Ellie? Dr Miller says there's a letter in the post for you about the whole thing. It looks as if there's something in those dreams you've been having."

And there was, for the very next morning, Ellie received another letter from Dr Miller.

Dear Ellie,

Congratulations on your exciting discovery of the ancient body in County Donegal. I am writing to tell you what we have already learnt from our forensic investigations and will keep you in touch as the body offers up more clues as to his identity.

The body is that of a young man, probably aged between 15 and 30, approximately 170 cm tall (5 ft 7 in) and about 56 kilos (9 stone). He had a full head of hair, probably shoulder-length or longer, and yellow in colour although this could be due to the destruction of darker pigment by the peat. He had little facial hair though there is evidence that the hairs on his upper lip had been recently trimmed with scissors. Of the full normal set of 32 teeth, the body had 28, that is to say he had no wisdom teeth, so it is likely that the body was that of a man at the younger end of the 15-30 range. The acidity of the peat has eroded the tooth enamel so it is impossible to say if dental decay was present.

The body was well-clothed, suggesting a person of some social standing. He had a thick woollen coat, thigh length, waisted, with long sleeves. His trousers, also of a woollen material, were wide and baggy, and gathered at the knee. On his feet were leather bootees with laces but these were badly decomposed. He also wore a narrow silver bracelet on his right wrist.

The body is well-built, apparently healthy, if somewhat underweight for his height, and showing no signs of disease. However, examinations by medical and forensic experts prove beyond doubt that the bogman met a violent death.

His injuries reveal that he was struck from behind

*twice on the top of his head with an axe-like weapon. A
further vicious blow to his back, possibly a violent kick,
broke one of his ribs. He was then dropped face
downwards into a pool in the bog where he was found.
For complete preservation to have taken place,
conditions at the time must have been anaerobic, (free
of oxygen) so the body must have sunk to the bottom of a
boggy pool and settled on the bottom.*

*Over time the physical geography of the area changed,
the pools on the bog disappeared and a firmer surface
developed near the cliff which eventually was covered
with heather. Coastal erosion in that area has noticeably
increased in the last hundred years; much of the
headland has already fallen into the sea and in view of
recent storm damage which has taken place there, it is
very likely that the location of the bogman's body would
have been lost within a very short time. Indeed, I would
hazard a guess that if you had not found the body, it
would have fallen into the sea this winter, so well done!*

*We were very excited to discover a broad sword lying
beneath the body. It is double-edged, made of iron, and
its hilt, or handle, is gilded. At one time it would have
been elaborately inlaid with stones although most of these
have been lost. The sword is in two pieces and is to be the
subject of further investigation, not least to see if the
sword had been broken deliberately but also because
there is an inscription along the length of the blade
which, we hope, we will be able to decipher.*

*Now you will surely want to know who this man was.
His name, of course, we can never know, but we have
been able to draw several conclusions about his identity.
With techniques like pollen-dating and carbon-dating,
we have been able to determine that the body is*

approximately one thousand years old. From our knowledge of contemporary costume, weaponry, and together with your other finds of the small silver coin and the antler comb* (although these were not found in close proximity to the body), I think we may conjecture that this man belonged to a Viking tribe which may have taken temporary refuge on the shores of Lough Foyle.

Ellie laid the letter on the dressing-table and walked over to the bedroom window. She felt a huge sense of relief. All the haunting dreams of the past winter made sense now. She had not imagined any of it. Harald *had* existed. He had come to Lough Foyle and there met his terrible fate. Perhaps she could never prove to anyone that the body they had found was her Harald, or that he had sailed from Bergen with his father Olaf of the Nine Sea-Battles. But it was enough that she knew, and that she had found him before the last remaining trace of the Vikings that had come to Lough Foyle fell and were dashed to pieces in the sea beneath the cliff. Harald, his poor old bones saved from watery disintegration, unseen and unmourned, would have some peace now. He would no longer have any need to be a walker after death, tending his own grave.

A few weeks later, Ellie and her mother made the journey to Dublin where they had been invited to visit the Viking Bogman before it went on public display. She could hardly contain her excitement. For weeks it had seemed that her secret world of Harald had been snatched away and taken over by interfering adults – the newspapers had been full of stories about The Bogman of Inishowen for days – so that her own image of

Harald was fading away like an over-exposed photograph. She had even begun to doubt all that he had told her and shown her in her dreams and in the hauntings. He had not appeared since the day she had found his body, perhaps because now he had no further use for her. She had done all she could for him. She pictured him, lying on a cold slab in a distant medical laboratory, prodded and gawped at by strangers, and spoke to him, more in hope than conviction, sending out waves of comfort to him so that he would know she was coming.

Chapter 11

Bogan, boggart, bocan, bodach, bogey-beasts, boggle
boos, bogies, bogles, bogy, bugan, buggane, bugs, bug-
a-boos, boggle boos, bog bears.

Dictionary of Fairies, Briggs, 1977

Ellie walked alongside Dr Miller down endless high-
windowed corridors which smelled strongly of
chemicals and disinfectant. Her mother followed behind,
flanked by two men in white coats whose names and
jobs she had not understood. They went through fire
door after fire door, then down steps into a basement
where their footsteps echoed on the stone floor.

"I believe you were up on the headland looking for a
lost bicycle the day you stumbled on the body?" said Dr
Miller.

"Yes," said Ellie, ignoring her mother's heavy sigh.
That was the story she had decided on and she wasn't
going to change it now.

"Well, it was a lucky thing for us that you lost it
then," Dr Miller went on. "This is one of the most intact
ancient bodies ever discovered in Ireland, so we are all
very excited about it. And of course it is the only bog

body from the Viking period."

"Were the other ones older or more recent?" Ellie asked.

"Most Irish bog bodies turn out to be from the late Middle Ages, though some are much older, probably about two thousand years old. We know of about eighty bodies altogether but there were almost certainly many other discoveries in bogs in earlier times that were never reported – until quite recently, people had no interest in archaeology. If they found something, they would just take anything valuable from the grave and cover up the body again. Nowadays of course we have the scientific knowledge to discover much more about these corpses and we can often establish how they died."

"Did anybody ever find any other bodies in Derry or Donegal?" Ellie interrupted.

"Funnily enough, the last bog body to turn up was also in Donegal. Turf-cutters came across it about fifteen years ago. It turned out to be a woman who had been buried wrapped up in the sort of woollen cloak which was worn in the later Middle Ages – but your body is several hundreds of years older than that."

"You said that this Viking that Ellie found was murdered?" Ellie's mother asked.

"Oh, there's no doubt about that at all. I'll show you how we know that in a moment." Dr Miller replied.

"And you can really be sure he was a Viking?" This was what Ellie most wanted to know. She had no doubt in her mind that the body they had found was Harald but it thrilled her so much that Dr Miller could confirm all that she had been dreaming about for months.

"Yes, indeed. One of the ways we can tell how old it is is by a process called carbon-dating. I was telling your friend Matt McLoughlin about a body that was found fairly recently in Cheshire in England – Lindow Man, he was called officially, although the papers nicknamed him Pete Marsh!" Dr Miller chuckled. "Well, shortly before the Lindow Man himself was found, another skull had been dug up in the same area. Now, this is the funny thing, there was a local man who was suspected of having murdered his wife and when the police confronted him about the discovery of the skull, he made a full confession and told them that he had indeed buried her up on the bog. But when the skull was sent off to the lab to be carbon-dated, it turned out to be from the Roman period – two thousand years old. That was the first time a body was carbon-dated in Britain."

"And it can be that precise?" asked Ellie. "You can be really sure this body is about a thousand years old?"

"Pretty sure – and we can fill in the picture from the clothes and the bracelet he was wearing which were typical of Viking costume. And the sword, of course, but that's another story. The coat is in a very bad state of repair but we can tell it was woollen and have a good idea of its design."

"Do you think there are more bodies like this still undiscovered?"

"Oh yes, wherever there is peat, there are bound to be finds – and not just bodies. The museum already has hundreds of items, leather shoes, tools, jewellery, all found down the centuries by men working on bogs in every part of Ireland, north and south. People have always known that bogs are strange places, a bit magical and a bit sinister – all over Ireland you'll hear stories of apparitions and strange happenings on bogs that would make horses rear in fright or men's hair stand on end. Bogey-men, boggles and boggarts – there are lots of names for fairies and ghosts and devils that all have something to do with bogs. Anyway, here we are," said the professor, stopping in front of a laboratory door. "Come and meet your Viking warrior. I don't think you'll find him a bit frightening."

Ellie stood in front of a long table and watched as the professor pulled back the sheeting. Behind her, she heard her mother gasp with surprise as the back of Harald's head was uncovered. For a moment Ellie too was shocked for the body was not at all what she had been expecting to see.

In front of her lay not the fair blond-haired young man who had haunted her dreams but a brown leathery-looking back. The man was lying face down, his head turned to one side and pressed down against his shoulder. His skin was a dark smoky brown colour as if he had been cured, and the body itself, what she could see of it, was squashed and flattened.

"I didn't expect it, I mean him, to look like this," said Ellie's mother. "I thought it would have been more like a skeleton."

"That's the effect of the peat, you see," said Dr Miller. "It preserves the soft tissue too."

"But look," said Ellie, with a rush of tenderness for Harald's poor old body, "you can still make out his eyelashes and eyebrows."

She moved closer. It was astonishing that a body so old could still be so identifiable, so human. One hand was just visible, peeping out from his right-hand side. He had long slim fingers with short rounded finger-nails. Could this really be the body of the man who had haunted her dreams? The same man who had so recently stood by her bedroom window and looked down at the River Foyle in flood? She could still clearly remember the exact tone of the voice telling her *Only you will know where to find me*. And she *had* found him. Why would she have dreamt of a Viking, why would she then have *found* a Viking, if they were not one and the same person. No, there was no doubt in her mind: this was Harald, son of Olaf of the Nine Sea-Battles, grandson of Harald, the blacksmith who had forged the best swords in Bergen. She reached out and gently laid her hand on his. As she touched him, she could hear his voice speak directly to her, *Only you knew where to find me*. No, she thought, you found me too. We both crossed an invisible border to reach one another.

Behind her, the others were talking in low voices.

"So far, we've removed the peat from his entire upper body but there is still a lot of work to be done," one of the men in the white coats was saying. "From x-rays and other investigations, we can tell his body is doubled up but it's more or less intact."

"Have you any idea about how he came to be there?" asked Ellie's mother.

"Bogs have always been treacherous, dangerous places," said Dr Miller, "the kind of place where men might stray off the beaten track and fall victim to drownings or robberies."

"But you said that in your letter that Har . . . that this man was killed," Ellie interrupted.

"Yes, we can be certain of that. Look here." The professor guided Ellie's hand to the crown of Harald's head to show her the two deep wounds.

"These are typical of the kind of injury caused by blows from a blunt weapon, one blow followed by another, with the victim struck from behind. The blows would have knocked him unconscious but the poor chap, whoever he was, may not have died instantly. There was swelling around the edges of the wounds so that means the man survived long enough for the swelling to develop. There's a rib fracture as well, that we think must have been caused by another heavy blow, maybe with some sort of truncheon or perhaps even a kick from behind. Then his killer, or killers, threw the body into a shallow boggy pool where it must have sunk to the bottom."

It was just as Harald had told her.

"But why did his body not rot away?"

"Obviously it was not exposed to air or warmth. In fact, because the body is so well preserved, we imagine the weather must have been very cold at the time of his death."

Yes, thought Ellie. It was midwinter. She remembered Harald's voice telling her: *Winter came early that year. There was a great snowfall and such cold that the very birds were falling out of the sky.*

She stroked the side of Harald's leathery face with her index finger.

"I have never seen a dead body before," she said, but even as she uttered the words, she remembered bodies lying on country roads that she had seen on television news, and bodies being carried away on stretchers by ambulance men and plastic body bags among the rubble-strewn aftermath of bombings in towns where she had gone shopping with her parents. An unending series of violent deaths down all the years.

"You don't think he was killed as some kind of sacrifice, do you?" asked Ellie's mother.

Ellie shuddered, remembering the great sacrifice of animals in honour of the god Frey, and the lust for blood that drove the Norsemen to take Harald's life.

"That body in England that was found back in the early eighties, wasn't he sacrificed?" her mum was saying.

"Lindow Man, you mean. Yes, he was garrotted," answered the professor very matter-of-factly. "Human sacrifice was practised in the Iron Age throughout Europe. There have been several bog bodies found in Denmark whose deaths were so violent we may be sure that the victims were either executed or sacrificed. One had his throat cut, another had a rope around his neck and had probably been strangled. And there is a case in England, the Burwell Fen Man, where the corpse was dressed in a belted leather coat, and was found standing upright in a dug-out canoe, clearly buried in some kind of ritual."

"But none in Ireland?" asked Ellie, remembering poor Gudrun the slave girl who was burnt alive with her master Olaf. No trace of her remained. Did anyone even know such things happened?

"We do have one Irish bog body from Galway who may have been sacrificed," said one of the men in white coats. "He is about two thousand years old and had been buried naked except for a deerskin cape. The remarkable thing was he had been pinned to the base of the bog with two wooden stakes – probably so that his soul could not be freed."

Ellie stroked the back of Harald's head, fingering the wounds left by the cowardly attack upon him.

"But, as far as this man is concerned," Dr Miller continued, "we believe he was simply murdered, rather than sacrificed. It seems he was just set upon from behind for whatever motive. If he had been sacrificed in some sort of ritual killing, you see, he would have been buried differently. The body would have been deliberately positioned to face east and west and his weapons and belongings placed carefully next to him."

"I agree," said one of the other men. "This was simply murder, murder most foul."

A heavy silence fell on everyone, broken only by the hum of the equipment that was controlling the temperature and humidity of the room. They all turned to look at Harald lying on the examination table, his long face twisted to one side. Her mother reached over and put her hand on Ellie's arm.

"Poor man," she said. "I don't suppose we can ever tell who he was and what he was doing in such a lonely place?"

Ellie felt a lump growing in her throat and swallowed hard. "I won't cry, Harald," she said to herself.

"Well, it's funny you should ask that, Mrs Mc Loughlin," said Dr Miller, "because we have something else very interesting to show you and Ellie. Something quite extraordinary."

Dr Miller ushered them through into an adjoining room, barely furnished but for bookcases stacked high with bundles of manila files and one long table. Dr Miller opened a long drawer and laid out on the table a large sheet of paper with a drawing of a long broad-bladed sword with an elaborate carved handle studded with precious stones.

"One of my research students drew that for you so you would have an idea of what it looked like when it was new – this is how it was when we found it under the body."

Dr Miller drew out the two pieces of the broken

sword and placed them in front of Ellie.

"It's a very high quality weapon, superbly made. Do you see these raised markings down the side of the blade – we call it runic writing? Well, they have been deciphered by the Department of Scandinavian Studies and we are tremendously excited by this discovery. It may back up our hypothesis that the body was one of the Viking fleet from Norway that is mentioned in the *Annals of Ulster* for the year 930 AD. The fleet was routed by the local kings but some of the Norsemen settled briefly in Inishowen in a place called Cen-rig. We don't know where that was exactly but it would have been somewhere on the shoreline of Lough Foyle in Inishowen, possibly the same place you found the body. Perhaps this man was even one of that group."

"What do the marks mean? Are they words?" asked Ellie, when she could get a word in.

Dr Miller guided her hand along the runic marks on the blade of the sword.

"It says simply, *I Harald of Bergen Made This Sword.*"

Ellie felt a cold shiver run down her spine. "Harald of Bergen," she repeated, not trusting herself to say any more. Her head was spinning and her heart was pounding so violently against her ribs she thought everyone must hear it. Suddenly everything was falling into place. She smiled broadly at everyone in the room, hugging her secret close to herself for how could she tell them all that she knew, all that Harald himself had revealed to her in his hauntings. Nobody but she would ever know, for she could and would not tell them, that this was not the Harald who made the sword, but his grandson. Nor would she tell them how the fleet had stopped at Cen-rig to bury Harald's father, Olaf of the

Nine Sea-Battles, or how they had chosen the site at the cliff where the raven of Odin had appeared. Nor would they ever know how, gradually, the berserks and the other sailors had deserted young Harald, believing him to have been cursed by the evil wolf Fenri, leaving him with only one small straggling band to found their new settlement, and how later, driven by hunger and jealousy and maddened by bad omens like the giant woman washed up on the shore, these same men had turned upon Harald and killed him. She would not tell them because they would not believe her and she could not bear Harald's story to be dismissed like that.

What had become of his killers, she wondered? Had they taken to the *Sleipnir* and returned to Bergen?

"Poor Harald, even you don't know what happened after they murdered you so I shall never know," she said inwardly to the cold stiff body.

"What will become of him now?" she asked the archaeologist.

"Oh, your Viking is immortal now. I expect he'll be in great demand from all sorts of scientists – and not just here in Ireland."

"So he need have no fear of being forgotten again."

"Not at all, there will be books written about him and probably TV programmes and people coming to the museum to marvel at him."

Ellie walked back to the table where the hunched body lay, its frail eyelashes resting upon a leathery cheek. Laying her hand on his, she spoke silently to him, "Now Harald, you are free. You have no need to be a walker-after-death any more. You told me where to look and I found you. Now I wish you peace."

And it seemed to Ellie that, for one moment, the body on the table became whole again; the limbs lengthened, the flattened head became long and slim and handsome, the hair grew thick and blond and Harald was as young and handsome as he had been all those years ago and as she had known him in her dreams.

That evening, the North-West was hit with a storm so violent it will be remembered for years to come. Roofs were blown off houses. Trees came crashing down, blocking roads and felling telegraph poles. On docksides, berthed ships were thrown up against sea walls, tearing gaping holes in the quays. Small fishing-boats were torn from their moorings and carried off out to sea. The straggling band of hippies in their mobile homes beside the coast woke to feel their houses lurch and slide beneath them and finally had the good sense to flee, leaving all their belongings behind them. Up at the site where Harald's body had been found, the ground began to tear and rip apart as the sea hurled itself against the cliff. Mr McLoughlin, lying sleepless in his old cottage at the top of the village, listened to the wind howling around his chimney stack and waited for the crash that he knew must surely come. Shortly after midnight, the place where Harald had lain so uneasily for over one thousand years gave up its unequal struggle with the sea and toppled in slow motion into the cold cold ocean.

At home in her bed in Derry, Ellie awoke with a start and sat bolt upright. The figure of Harald stood by her window, smiling at her with his piercing blue eyes, calmer and happier than she had ever seen him.

You found me, Ellie, he said. *Now I have my peace.*

Bibliography

Chapter 1   Extract from the *Annals of Ulster*, Vol. I
             (431-1056) ed. Wm. Hennessy, HMSO
             Dublin, 1887

Chapter 3   *New Complete Geography 1*, Charles Hayes,
             Gill & Macmillan, 1989

Chapter 4   *The Princess*, Prologue, Alfred Lord
             Tennyson

Chapter 5   Extract from *Medieval Irish Lyrics*, James
             Carney, p. xxx, Dolmen Press, 1985

Chapter 6   Extract from poem, Storm at Sea, Anon,
             trans. Frank O' Connor, *The Penguin Book
             of Irish Verse*, ed. Brendan Kennelly, 1970

Chapter 7   Contemporary eyewitness account of a Viking
             cremation quoted in *The Vikings*, Johannes
             Brondsted, Penguin, 1960

Chapter 8   Extract from the *Annals of Ulster*, ibid.

Chapter 9   Extract from article "Irish Bog Bodies", Raghnall
             Ó Floinn, *Archaeology*, Vol. 2 No 3, Autumn,
             1988

Chapter 10   *Of the Bogs and Loughs of Ireland*, W King,
             Philosophical Transactions of the Royal Society,
             1685

Chapter 11   *Dictionary of Fairies*, Wm. Briggs, Penguin, 1977

Also by Poolbeg

Charlie's Story

By

Maeve Friel

Abandoned by her mother at Victoria Station, London, at the age of four, Charlotte 'Charlie' Collins is sent to live with her father in Dublin.

Now fourteen, Charlie struggles to come to terms with the reasons for her mother's desertion, her father's silence and the cruelty of her classmates.

In this terrifying tale about school bullying, Charlie learns that her individuality is also her strength.

Intense, disturbing and deeply moving, Maeve Friel's book is a harrowing account of like on the edge and one girl's determination to turn her life around.

Also by Poolbeg

Shiver!

An atmospheric and suspense-filled collection of
original ghost stories by fifteen of Ireland's most
popular writers including Rose Doyle, Michael Scott,
Maeve Friel, Jane Mitchell, Michael Mullen,
Morgan Llywelyn and Cormac MacRaois.

*What became of the hideous voodoo doll Niamh flung
from her bedroom window?*

*Witness a family driven quietly insane by an evil
presence in their new house . . .*

*Read about Lady Margaret de Deauville who was
murdered in 1814 and discover the power of her
magic ring . . .*

*Who is the ghoulish knight who clambers out of his
tomb unleashing evil power on the world?*

*Discover the identity of the disembodied voice singing
haunting tunes in the attic of a long abandoned
house . . .*

Each tale draws you into a web at times menacing, at
times refreshingly funny.

Also by Poolbeg

The Hiring Fair

By

Elizabeth O'Hara

It is 1890 and Parnell is the uncrowned king of
Ireland. But thirteen-year-old Sally Gallagher,
"Scatterbrain Sally" as her mother and younger sister
Katie call her, has no interest in politics. She is happy
to read books and leave the running of the house to
those who like housework.

A shocking tragedy changes the lives of the sisters.
Instead of being the daughters of a comfortable
Donegal farmer and fisherman, they have to become
hired servants, bound for six months to masters they
don't know.

Elizabeth O'Hara has written an exciting story that has
its share of sorrow and joy. She creates in Scatterbrain
Sally a new and unforgettable Irish heroine.

Also by Poolbeg

Blaeberry Sunday

By

Elizabeth O'Hara

*That summer had changed the
course of her life for ever:
"Was every little thing that happened
as significant as every other little
thing in shaping the course of
a person's life?"*

The summer leading up to Blaeberry Sunday –
the festival of Lughnísí – in 1893 was the hottest
and driest anyone in Donegal had ever
experienced. Determined not to remain a hired girl
for the rest of her days, Sally returns to Glenbra
only to witness an eviction, death, and the
courtship of her mother and Packy Doherty, a local
farmer. Nothing, however, is quite so devastating
as her love for Manus McLoughlin and the events
preceding that fateful Blaeberry Sunday.